New York Times and *U* ...
Daire St. Denis is an a ...
history addict, a seasor ...
She calls the Canadian Rockies home, and has the
best job ever: writing smoking-hot contemporary
romance in which the pages are steeped in sensuality
and there's always a dash of the unexpected. Find out
more about Daire and subscribe to her newsletter at
dairestdenis.com.

If you liked *Pleasure Games*, why not try

Burn Me Once by Clare Connelly
Boardroom Sins by J. Margot Critch
Legal Attraction by Lisa Childs

Discover more at millsandboon.co.uk

PLEASURE GAMES

DAIRE ST. DENIS

MILLS & BOON

First Published in Great Britain 2018
by Mills & Boon, an imprint of HarperCollins*Publishers*
1 London Bridge Street, London, SE1 9GF

© 2018 Dara Lee Snow

ISBN: 978-0-263-93218-8

MIX
Paper from
responsible sources
FSC® **C007454**

This book is produced from independently certified FSC™ paper
to ensure responsible forest management.
For more information visit www.harpercollins.co.uk/green.

Printed and bound in Spain
by CPI, Barcelona

For Steena, Elena and Trish.
True friendships are where sanity and insanity collide.

CHAPTER ONE

LUCA LEGRAND COULDN'T decide whether he had the best luck in the world or whether he was actually cursed with the worst fucking luck ever. At the moment, sitting in a holding cell that stank like piss and rancid sweat, he was pretty sure it was the latter.

"Legrand!" A uniformed member of the Paris Police Prefecture banged on the bars. *"Votre avocat est ici."* Your lawyer is here.

Pushing himself to his feet, Luca waited for the man to unlock the cell and then followed him down the hall to a cubicle not much larger than a toilet stall. François Chevalier, the lawyer for the Legrand Estate vineyard, was already waiting inside, reading a newspaper at a steel table that was bolted to the floor.

François glanced up when the door opened. He didn't stand, and did not greet Luca, but rather drummed his fingers on the metal tabletop as he waited for Luca to take the seat across from him.

Once the door was shut behind the officer, François went back to reading the paper. More specifically, he perused an article with the headline, Héritier de Legrand Vineyard en Prison Pour Voies de Fait. *Heir to the Legrand Vineyard in Prison for Assault.* Beneath the headline was a blown-up image of Luca being shoved into a police car.

"It's not as bad as it looks," Luca said.

"Really? Because it looks bad," François said calmly, though his mustache twitched.

Luca leaned back in the hard metal chair, folding his arms over his chest. He gazed directly at François, not willing to look away because he was not contrite in the fucking least.

"It's not my fault," he said.

"Is that so?" François leaned toward him, palms on the table, forcing Luca to look up at him. His face—though always red—was now the color of a sun-ripened heirloom tomato. "You punched a reporter. You broke his nose. You smashed his camera. How is that *not* your fault?"

He stood up and swept a hand around the tiny room that smelled like mildew and stale cigarettes. "The first Legrand man to ever be arrested. Yet still you sit there and say it's not your fault?" He made a sour face, as if tasting a too-green wine, one that should be spit out immediately.

Slowly, Luca got to his feet, all six feet two inches of him, so François had to look up at *him*. "The man deserved what he got."

"I don't care what he deserved. All I care about is your legacy. Which you have single-handedly destroyed." He glared at Luca. His heavy lids and the bags beneath made it nearly impossible to see his eyes, but Luca was determined to hold François's gaze. The fact that François looked away first did not give him any pleasure, however.

"The value of our champagne has dropped significantly since you took over. Do you realize that?"

Luca ground his teeth, forcing himself to count to five. *Un, deux, trois, quatre, cinq...* But counting did not stop the deepest part of his gut from rumbling with liquid fire that was amplified with every breath. Through clenched teeth, he said, "The value of our champagne dropped the day my father died."

It was true. His father had run the estate for thirty years, continuing in the footsteps of his father and grandfather and two hundred years of ancestors before that. His father had been a robust, healthy man and it had seemed as if he would live forever. Not that Luca had seen much of him in the past ten years while he was competing on the Grand Prix motorcycle racing circuit.

"This cannot continue—" François gestured toward Luca's chest. "These scandals."

Here we go. Luca leaned against the wall, crossing one ankle over the other. Waiting for François to detail each of his latest "scandals." There was no point in defending himself.

Ticking items off his finger, François began the lengthy list. "Disturbing the peace."

Disturbing the peace? Luca had broken up with his girlfriend, Anika Van Horn, a model he'd quickly learned was more interested in the fame and fortune of the Legrand name than in Luca himself. She did not take the breakup well. In fact, she'd slapped him, making sure to do so at an outdoor café, causing a scene that spread in seconds via social media. He still wasn't sure how charges had come of it.

"Public drunkenness."

He had attended a fellow Monster teammate's bachelor party. While Luca had had his fair share of drinks, he had not been nearly as drunk as the groom-to-be, whom Luca had rescued from the Fontaine Stravinsky.

"Public nudity."

It had been his friend, the bachelor, who was naked. But the press had a way of spinning things so that it sounded like Luca was the one who'd disrobed, jumped into the fountain and done lewd things to a colorful, busty mermaid with water spouting from the tips of her breasts.

Sighing, Luca waved for François to keep going with the damning list, knowing what was coming next.

"Then. Just to up the ante…a sex video gone public. And not just any sex…" François paused, arching his brow for effect. He sniffed instead of finishing his sentence. "Such a boost to the prestige of your esteemed family name." François grimaced with sarcasm.

Luca opened his mouth, the excuse—the fact that the video was meant to be private and that Anika had obviously been the one to leak it online, either for publicity to boost her career or to publicly humiliate him—was ripe on his tongue. But what good would it do to explain this to François? It didn't change the outcome.

"And now, one week later, here you are." François's eyes leaked with moisture born of anger, like a grape in the press right before it was about to pop. "Assault and destruction of property. How noble."

The paparazzi had been relentless since the sex scandal. Luca had been unable to leave his flat. To go to the market. To do anything without being accosted. When one particularly pushy reporter, who had been doggedly harassing him night and day, had stepped in front of Luca while he was on his brand new Yamaha VMAX, causing him to swerve and nearly crash into a lamppost, Luca had lost it. He wasn't proud of his actions, but if faced with the same situation again? He wouldn't change a thing.

He'd parked the bike, walked straight up to the man who had the camera attached to his face like it was an appendage and asked him—civilly—to erase the images. When the man ignored him in order to take more pictures, Luca had simply snatched the camera away with the intent to erase the memory. The man shoved him, which resulted in Luca dropping the camera, smashing it on the cobblestones.

Oops.

Then the screaming idiot had thrown a punch, which Luca had easily dodged before acting on pure instinct. One punch. That's all it took to drop the *petit connard*. It wasn't his fault the man had started something he couldn't finish.

Again. No point in explaining any of this to François. The man cared about one thing and one thing only. The value of the estate. Which had, indeed, plummeted since Luca took over.

"I get it." Luca returned to the chair and sat down. "I'm a big fucking disappointment. Now, when are you bailing me out of this shit hole so I can get to work to rebuild the 'family name'?"

"Bail you out?" François laughed. "I'm not bailing you out. *Non*." He shook his head. "This is the safest place for you. You can't get into any more trouble if you stay locked up."

The molten metal that swirled in his gut erupted, filling Luca's veins, forcing every muscle to contract.

He grabbed François by the collar and hauled him across the table toward him. "What did you say?"

The only sound François was able to manage was a sputtering plea for his release, which resulted in spittle spraying Luca in the face. For the first time that day, Luca felt remorse for his actions. François had been loyal to the family for three decades, yet he barely knew Luca, and for all he did know, Luca was indeed the fuckup that the media was making him out to be.

The sex scandal was one thing, but Luca couldn't understand the rest of it—the charges and the constant bad press. As a Grand Prix driver and a Legrand, he was used to being in the public eye, but lately the media seemed out to get him. Why? Was it because of the sex tape, or did he simply keep ending up in the wrong place at the wrong time?

Softening his grip, Luca raised his hands in appeasement. "I'm sorry."

"Sorry?" François's voice was high. "This behavior of yours is unacceptable." The lawyer straightened his shirt and tie where Luca had crumpled it. "You are an embarrassment to your family name."

"François, I recognize the…" Luca swallowed. With difficulty. "The *folly* of my recent actions. But I can't very well right wrongs from a prison cell."

Blinking rapidly, his eyes so puffy they were mere slits in his face, François said, "I don't think you understand the full implications of your actions."

"Then explain them to me."

François removed a sheaf of papers from a briefcase beneath the table and plopped them on the table.

"Do you know what these are?"

Luca slid the papers toward him. "Company by-laws." He slid them back across.

"Yes. And, if you were to read them, you would know that there is a code of conduct clause." He paused. "For *all* employees." He flipped to an earmarked page and shoved the document back across the table.

Luca glanced down. The words "grounds for dismissal" were highlighted as well as, "appropriate conduct."

"I know the bylaws. I am the CEO." It was sort of true. He'd been too busy running the company to pay much attention to them.

"So it should come as no surprise that the board is discussing your removal as CEO."

"What?" Luca guffawed. "They can't do that. I'm the only heir to the estate and I own fifty-one percent of the shares of the company."

"Well…"

"Well, what?"

"There has been discussion about your father's will being contested. In light of all that has occurred." He gestured toward the room in general.

"Contested? By whom?"

"Marcel Durand."

Marcel was only a few years younger than Luca and had only worked for his father for maybe five years. "Why would Marcel Durand contest *my* father's will?"

"Because Marcel is your half brother."

The first thing Jasmine Sweet did after finding her seat in first class on the Air France flight to Paris was to ask for a glass of champagne. The second thing she did, once she had the glass in hand, was to turn away from the large and empty seat beside her and sip the bubbly liquid until it disappeared. And the third thing she did was twist off the platinum band with the four-carat princess-cut diamond and shove it into the inside pocket of her purse. This was all accomplished before the plane had finished boarding.

"Excuse me." Jasmine held up a finger to signal the unfairly beautiful and terribly refined French flight attendant. "Do you have any berries? Blueberries, raspberries, that sort of thing?"

"Berries?" The woman asked with what Jasmine decided was a disdainful tone. *"Non."*

"Too bad. Just another champagne, then, please."

The woman pursed her lips before settling into a bored smile. "Would you care for orange juice with that or perhaps something to eat?"

"No, thank you," Jazz said, waving her hand dismissively. "Just the champagne."

Before the attendant moved past, Jasmine stopped her again. "Oh, and if it's not too much to ask…" Jasmine glanced at the seat beside her and lowered her voice. "This seat is empty." She pulled tickets out of her purse. "I have both tickets. Would you see if someone from economy would be interested in an upgrade?"

Both delicate brows arched at this request as the woman took the tickets from Jasmine's hands. Her full lips pursed together. "Yes, I see." Handing the tickets back to Jasmine, she said, "I will inquire."

"Oh, and make sure they like champagne. That's a must," Jasmine called, but the woman didn't turn around. "Thanks," she shouted. "You're a peach."

The flight attendant carried on through into coach,

ignoring her while she made sure all carry-on items were stowed correctly.

Well, what had she expected? Friendliness? Kindness? Empathy?

Ha! So far her experience with the French was that they were aloof, intimidating and gorgeous. But, she supposed, she wasn't even off American soil yet. Things would be better once she landed in Paris.

She rubbed the bare spot where her ring had been only moments before. Her skin was lighter where the band had circled her finger for the last sixteen months, a promise of the life she'd always dreamed of, as if her skin wasn't quite ready to give it up.

She closed her eyes, imagining that she and Parker Wright had gotten married yesterday, as planned, celebrating their union at the Waldorf Astoria in Chicago with three hundred of their closest friends and family—Parker had a large family. And lots of friends. Well… work colleagues and friends of his parents, really. But whatever. And now they were on their way to Europe for their honeymoon. With eyes closed, she observed the physical sensation of the plane taxiing along the runway before accelerating, the seat beneath her vibrating as the plane took off.

A week in Paris, another week in the South of France, then on to Italy: Venice, Milan, Tuscany—ahh!—before returning to Paris for the final few days. She'd planned the whole thing, poring over hotel web pages and travel forums for what to do and where to stay.

"Money's no problem," Parker had said. "It's our honeymoon, after all."

Yes. It was their honeymoon and she'd booked all

these gorgeous boutique hotels close to the sights, restaurants and shops—shopping was something they both loved to do. And then, after a day of exploring, she'd thought they would return to their hotel and make love—tenderly, passionately. Definitely trying new things now that they were married (like the new furry handcuffs she'd picked up and the ridged vibrator—yes, please!). As her imagination strayed to creative ways to use the toys, her hand strayed to the seat beside her, encouraging Parker to take her hand and clasp it in his warm fingers.

Instead, her hand came into contact with a large, hairy arm that was a smidge damp. Jasmine's eyes popped open and she swiveled to face the person seated beside her. He appeared to be in his late fifties or early sixties with thinning hair and a friendly face. He wore a tie-dyed T-shirt that stretched across an ample frame, and as he met her gaze, he pushed square glasses back onto the bridge of his nose before dipping his hand into a party-sized bag of Doritos. Jasmine noticed bright orange crumbs dotting the front of his shirt and the armrest.

"Doritos?" he asked, as he held the bag out to her.

"Don't mind if I do," Jasmine said, taking a handful. She waved at the glass of champagne sweating on her pull-down table. "Do you want something to drink? It's free up here, you know."

The man smiled and Jasmine tried not to stare at the orange residue stuck between his two front teeth. "Don't mind if *I* do."

Jazz pressed the button to signal the attendant and the woman materialized beside her seat. "Another champagne for my friend, here."

"I'd prefer beer if you don't mind."

"I don't mind." Jasmine smiled sweetly at the man before turning her beaming face toward the French woman. "Beer for my friend. And another champagne for me. In fact," Jazz added, indicating the first-class cabin with a wave of her hand, "Why don't you bring out champagne for everyone!"

The woman rolled her eyes but Jasmine didn't care. Was it the champagne making her feel light-headed and carefree?

"Toodle-oo, now." She motioned with just the tips of her fingers, hoping to give the woman—who wasn't even attempting the bored smile anymore—the brush-off. Then she turned to her seatmate.

"I'm Jasmine." Jazz stuck her hand out and the man beside her took it, shaking it with a surprisingly firm grasp.

"Neil."

"Nice to make your acquaintance, Neil. So, tell me about yourself."

The two exchanged pleasantries: where they were from, what they did for a living, whether they'd been to Paris before.

See? Jasmine consoled herself. *Look how calm I am, making nice with a complete stranger as if everything is normal.*

As if her whole world hadn't been turned upside down a mere forty-eight hours ago and she hadn't received the worst shock of her life.

Their drinks arrived, though Jasmine noticed her champagne was a little on the glass-half-empty side.

Bitch.

"So, Neil, what's in Paris? Business or pleasure?"

She downed the champagne in three swallows and pressed the call button again.

Two can play this game, gorgeous French woman.

"Oh, a comic convention. It's the biggest one in all of Europe. I'm an illustrator." He brushed a wisp of hair off his forehead.

"Interesting." Jasmine helped herself to another handful of Doritos. "What kind of illustrations?"

"Do you want to see?"

"Why not?"

Neil unfastened his seat belt and retrieved a bag from the overhead compartment, taking out a sketchbook before replacing the bag and sitting down. He flipped open the sketchbook to cartoons of—well, Jasmine was having a hard time focusing, to be honest.

"The cartoon is called Betty Boobs. It's a play on Betty Boop. It's very popular in Europe."

Jasmine blinked and squinted. Big-chested, naked cartoon women with a bit of 1930s flare graced the pages of his sketchpad. Getting it on. Porn. The guy drew cartoon porn.

Cool.

"Neil, can I ask you something?"

"Sure."

"Do you know what a beard is?" She blinked at him, forcing herself to swallow. That last sip of champagne had burned.

"You mean like facial hair?" He stroked his chin.

"No. The other connotation. Do you know it?"

His bushy brows drew together and then rose up his forehead as if filled with helium. "You mean like a gay guy who—"

"Yes." She poked him on the arm. "That's exactly

what I mean. For example, my fiancé—well, ex-fiancé—asked me to marry him, right?"

"Okay."

"Unbeknownst to me, I was his beard." Reaching over to the little table in front of Neil, Jasmine snagged the can of Bud that he'd barely sampled and guzzled a good third before continuing. "We were supposed to get married yesterday."

"Really?" His gaze was on the beer, not her.

She nodded.

Wow. She was really doing it. No tears. No temper tantrums. Just reporting the facts as if it had happened to someone else or like she was completely over it. Jasmine was proud of herself.

She drank deeply again before leaning close and placing her hand on Neil's sweating forearm. "Yep. I'd have never known, except the night before the wedding, while I was supposed to be staying at a hotel with my friends, I came back to my apartment to pick up something I'd forgotten—something borrowed, or was it something blue?" She tapped her lips. "Hmm. Either way, that part doesn't matter. What matters is that I caught my fiancé in bed with his best friend. They were booping. *Betty Booping*, if you will."

"Holy shit," Neil said, still eyeing the beer in her hand. "That must have been a shock."

"Oh, yeah." She pointed to the seat he was occupying. "My new husband was supposed to be sitting where you are sitting right now, but he's not. Because he's gay."

"I'm sorry."

"He never loved me." Jasmine fell back into her seat, staring at the headrest in front of her. "He was only using me. God. And I was so blind because he gave me whatever I wanted."

"Hey." The guy patted her hand where it lay on the shared armrest. "You okay?" He carefully retrieved his nearly empty beer from her slack fingers.

"A gorgeous penthouse apartment. Fifty-thousand-dollar limit on my credit card."

"I can't imagine…though a limit like that would be nice…"

"You know what the worst thing was, Neil?" She lolled her head toward him. "After I caught him? He was relieved. *Relieved.*"

"It's hard to live a lie, I guess…"

"And he said nothing had to change." She poked him in the sternum, above the orange crumbs. "Can you believe it? He still wanted to marry me!"

"Umm, you might want to keep it down a bit—"

"A housekeeper and cook if I wanted…whatever I wanted, really. Bribery." She shook her head. Her neck was stiff. So was her jaw. Tight, like it was wired shut. "All fucking bribes and distractions," she said through clenched teeth. "Distractions from what, you might ask?" She turned to face Neil and the rest of the story came out of the deep hole where her heart used to be. "So that *my* soon-to-be husband could take business trips with *Robert*. That's the fucker's name. *Robert Miskey*. I'm a fucking cover so Parker can be-boop Robert *fucking* Miskey."

"You're not allowed to shout on planes these days." Neil blinked nervously.

"Am I making a scene, Neil? Am I?"

"Umm, yes."

"Don't you think finding out that you're a beard on the eve of your wedding warrants a scene?"

The man was now frantically pushing the attendant call button.

Unbuckling her seat belt, Jasmine stood, addressing all the people in first class. "I'm supposed to be married. I'm supposed to be on my way to Europe for my honeymoon. And instead I'm here with Neil, who draws cartoon porn." She glanced at Neil and said in a marginally more controlled voice, "Sorry, Neil."

His smile wavered and his hands said, *No problem, crazy lady.*

"Doesn't that give me the right to make a scene?" She tried to meet the other passengers' eyes, but there were no takers. "Doesn't it?"

Cool fingers circled her upper arm and an accented voice said calmly, "Please return to your seat or we will be forced to make a stop in New York City where you will be escorted off the plane and detained. Do you understand?"

Jasmine attempted to tug her arm out of the attendant's grasp but the woman was freakishly strong. Fucking French.

"I—" When she turned her head she was met with the sincerest smile she'd received from the woman yet.

"Please," the woman said soothingly. Her sincerity came as such a surprise that Jasmine's knees buckled and the woman had to help her back into her seat.

Jazz caught a whiff of the woman's perfume—Coco Mademoiselle by Chanel, if she wasn't mistaken—as the flight attendant leaned over her to secure Jasmine's seat belt. Tasteful, subtle, perfect.

"I'm very sorry you're having a bad day. Please

don't make it any worse." Before standing, the woman
tucked a handful of tissues into Jasmine's fist and,
moving close to her ear, whispered, "Whoever this man
is who hurt you? He did not deserve you."

CHAPTER TWO

THE SECOND JASMINE opened the door to her hotel room, she smelled roses.

Ugh.

Towing her bag behind her like it was an old, arthritic dog who was too tired to go for a walk, Jasmine made her way through the suite she had so lovingly booked months ago. Months ago when she thought she'd be sharing this room with the man she was supposed to spend the rest of her life with. But he'd been lying to her the whole time! Asshole.

The room was gorgeous—dammit! Twelve-foot ceilings and original crown molding from when the hotel was a mansion owned by a famous jeweler who had bought it for his mistress during the Renaissance. Now the beautiful, airy suite only mocked her. The Louis XIV furniture taunted her, reminding her that she'd chosen it for Parker. She preferred country chic. The filmy white drapes only served to remind her of the ten-thousand-dollar wedding gown that hid in her closet like a shameful secret, never to be worn.

But the worst was what she found on the polished cherrywood table in the sitting area: a plate of chocolate-covered strawberries, with an envelope addressed to Mr. and Mrs. Parker Wright propped between the berries and an ice bucket. Inside the bucket was a bottle of champagne sitting at a jaunty angle, chillin'.

Like a villain.

Stupid champagne.

Jasmine plucked the bottle from the bucket, unwrapped the foil on top and popped the cork. It ricocheted off what she hoped was an imitation painting, then off the crown molding, landing somewhere behind a potted plant. Not bothering with the crystal flutes, Jasmine drank directly from the bottle like it was water and she was dying of thirst.

"Hair of the dog," she muttered, wiping her lips with the back of her hand. She set the bottle on the table, unconcerned with the wet patch left on the highly polished tabletop, and rummaged in her bag for aspirin. Instead of the travel-sized bottle of pills, she located her cell phone.

According to her phone it was 3:23 and there were forty-seven—yes, forty-seven!—texts waiting for her. Reminding her—as if she needed any more reminders—of the ordeal of the last forty-eight hours.

With a groan, she tapped the message app…

Five from her mother. Delete.

Two from her father. Delete.

Thirteen from her best friend, Ashley…hmm. Maybe she'd read those later.

Twenty-seven from Parker.

The man was desperate.

Her finger hovered over the delete button, but instead of deleting the messages, she deleted him from her contact list.

"Liar. You're dead to me," she muttered before tilting her head way back and letting the bubbly burn down her throat.

Parker's voice rose between her ears, *C'mon, Jazz. I figured you knew. Nothing has to change between us. I still love you, you know, as a best friend.* He'd made that statement while sitting in bed beside his lover. Then he'd gotten out of bed and approached her, hands out, pleading. *You can have whatever life you want, I won't interfere. All I ask is that you keep my private life secret.*

Honestly? In this day and age, why did he need to pretend? Well, she'd asked him that question directly.

It's my father. He's homophobic, okay? I'll lose the trust fund.

God! So, all of this was for the money? He'd deceived her for years just so he could maintain his precious lifestyle?

Not that she'd minded the lifestyle. It was what had kept her from making demands, from thinking too hard about the lack of intimacy and passion she'd yearned for. Parker's generosity seemed proof enough he loved her, and she'd been so wrapped up in their perfect life, she'd failed to see what was happening right in front of her.

With bottle in hand, Jasmine wove toward the window, pushing the drapes aside so she could admire the view.

And what a view. The rounded Parisian rooftops, the Eiffel Tower—so close she could practically lick it. The view was the reason Jasmine had chosen this suite, a dream come true…

Opening the French doors, Jasmine stepped out onto the wrought-iron balcony. Fresh air. That was what she needed. She plunked herself down in the chair and set the bottle on the glass-topped bistro table as she gazed out at the magnificent sight.

And she had no one to share it with. She was completely and utterly alone. She sighed, slumping with the weight of self-pity. Wasn't she allowed? She'd been ready to give Parker everything, thinking he'd felt the same way. She shut her eyes. Maybe her ex-fiancé cared for her, even loved her, like he'd said. But it wasn't the kind of love she'd thought it was. The love she'd always craved. And she wasn't ready to forgive him for tricking her into believing that it was. Her phone chirped, and Jasmine automatically glanced down. Another message from Ashley. Tapping on the message app, she skimmed the messages.

Jazz? Are you okay? Call me.
Please, let me know you're okay.
Your parents are worried. You should call them.
Jazz? Are you in Paris?

Instead of replying to the text, Jasmine touched the FaceTime button. Her best friend answered immediately. The video was grainy, but Jasmine could still see the dark circles beneath Ashley's hazel eyes and that her fine blond hair had yet to be combed.

"What time is it there?" Jasmine asked by way of a greeting.

Ashley blinked. "It's twenty to ten."

"In the morning?"

Ashley's eyes narrowed. "I knew it. You went to Paris, didn't you?"

"See for yourself," Jasmine said, panning her phone to give Ashley a panoramic view of the Paris skyline.

"Holy shit," she heard Ashley comment. "Nice."

Switching the screen back to face her, Jasmine half smiled. "It's nicer now that I have you to share it with." She sighed. Damn if her lip didn't start quivering. "If I had been thinking clearly, I would have changed the other ticket and brought you with me." Her lip quivered for real and she covered her mouth to quell the shaking.

"If you had been thinking clearly, you would have at least told me—told someone—what you were doing. Jesus, Jazz. We've been so worried."

"I know. I'm sorry. I just…" She had to stop talking because the trembling in her lips spread across her face, pricking the backs of her eyes until tears spilled over her lashes. She shook her head since words were impossible at the moment.

"Have you talked to Parker?" Ash asked softly.

"No." Jazz wiped her cheek with the back of her hand. "I'm not going to, either."

"Understandable. What about your parents?"

"I will." She passed back through the French doors into the hotel suite and plopped down at the table, plucking a sweating strawberry from the plate and popping it into her mouth.

"So, what are you going to do?" Ash asked. "God, those strawberries look good, by the way."

Jazz grabbed another berry and bit into it. "They are good. Really sweet." Her voice cracked on the last word and the chocolate-covered berry suddenly tasted like ashes in her mouth. She swallowed the lump with difficulty.

After a pause, Ashley piped up, "I'll tell you what you're going to do."

"What?"

"You are going to have yourself an adventure."

"An adventure?"

"Yep. You want to forget about Parker? Go have fun. Do all the things that you want to do. Shop on the Champs-Élysées, go on wine tours and see the sights. Hell, take a train to Monte Carlo and rack up Parker's credit cards."

Something hot yet icy lanced Jasmine's gut. "Oh, God. The credit cards." She shook her head vehemently. "I don't want to use them."

"What do you mean?" Ash asked, leaning closer to her phone camera. "After all you've been through? You deserve to spend some of Parker's money."

"No. I can't do it. I can't live off of him anymore. It's just so…" She squeezed her eyes shut. "Symbolic of my life with him. Dependent and lame."

Even from across the distance, Jasmine heard Ashley's deep inhalation, followed by a long exhalation. "But, how are you going to survive if you don't?"

The reminder that she had no way of supporting herself slammed through Jasmine. When she'd met Parker she'd been working as a stylist in an upscale salon. She'd liked the job—loved it, actually—but as her relationship with Parker progressed, they'd seen little reason for her to keep it. He made more than enough to support them.

"I don't know. I guess I didn't think about money before I left."

Ashley rubbed her jaw, her gaze sliding up and to

the side as she considered this possibility. Her gaze returned to the screen. "Where's the ring?"

"What ring?"

"Duh…your engagement ring?"

Jasmine's gaze automatically searched her ring finger only to find it bare. Her purse! She reached inside, found the cold platinum and held it in front of the phone for Ashley to see.

"Get rid of it."

"Like, chuck it?"

"No! That thing cost Parker a fortune. Go sell it. Use the money to do something wild and crazy. And whatever's left? That's what you use to start over."

Jazz held the ring up, seeing it in a new light. Could she do that?

Hell, yes, she could. The ring was *hers*. Parker had given it to her when he said he'd love her forever. Now she was heartbroken, fucked over and desperately in need of a break. Parker probably wouldn't even care.

Jazz bit her lip. "I'll sell the ring, but I don't know how to do 'wild and crazy'."

"Oh, my God." Ashley slapped her forehead. "I've known you most of my life and if there is anyone who knows how to be wild, it's you."

"Ash…"

"Don't Ash me. You know what you need?"

"A drink?" Jazz held the champagne bottle aloft.

"I think you've self-medicated enough," Ash replied with pursed lips. "No. Here's what you need. Go find yourself some smoking-hot Frenchman who knows how to treat a woman. And then you need to have a month of raunchy, nasty, awesome sex." She snapped her fingers. "A sex-venture."

"A sex-what?" Jasmine rolled her eyes.

"I'm not kidding. You need a release from all this tension—what better way than good sex? You're totally single now."

Jasmine groaned.

"I'm sorry, hon. But that's why you need a passionate, torrid, love affair. Feed some romantic French dude chocolate-covered strawberries. Let him lick champagne off your body…"

"Seriously?"

"Go to one of those sex districts and buy awesome European sex toys…or…" Ashley's eyes lit up. "No, wait! Buy yourself a gigolo. A super-hot one!"

Jazz couldn't help laughing at Ashley's suggestion. It felt good to laugh. "You are insane." She blew her bangs out of her eyes. "And you should be here," she finished softly.

"Yeah, well…" Ashley stood and patted her rounded belly. Her friend was tiny, so her third trimester of pregnancy made her look like she had a basketball tucked up under her shirt. "I'm not exactly in the best form for sex-ventures. Plus, I'm pretty sure I would scare off any potential hotties."

Jasmine touched her finger to the screen as if touching Ashley's belly. "That is one lucky kid to have you for her mother."

Ashley's lips twisted. Her friend had worries of her own with her first child due in under a month.

"Thanks, Ash."

"Hey. What are friends for? You know I'm here for you. Anytime. I'm just a FaceTime away."

Jazz nodded.

"Oh, and Jazz?"

"Yeah?"

"Let me be your cautionary tale…" Ash rubbed her belly. "As soon as you sell that ring and before you embark on your sexy time?"

Jazz groaned. "Uh-huh?"

"Buy condoms. Lots and lots of condoms."

Two weeks had passed since Luca had been released on bail. The agreement he'd made with François was that he'd not only stay out of the limelight, but that he'd disappear completely while François worked behind the scenes to change the board's mind. He had hired Myra Monte, publicity guru to the stars, to try to salvage the Legrand brand—promos, charity donations and the like.

"Give me a month," François had said. "During that time, I don't want to hear about you, read about you or have to bail you out."

"But wouldn't it be better if I talk to the board? Prove to them I'm competent?"

"No. You have to trust me."

Luca did trust him. Thus he was lying low, as requested, staying out of the press, staying out of trouble. The problem was, scandal had followed him for the last year like a stray dog he'd fed on a whim, a dog that wouldn't leave him alone. It was that feral beast he didn't trust.

Bad luck? Luca wasn't so sure anymore.

He stopped his Ducati Diavel Cruiser at the red light, considering for the thousandth time the information François had revealed.

What if he was being sabotaged? If he was, Luca knew exactly who was behind it.

Marcel Durand. His half brother.

Luca still had a hard time processing the news. Marcel was blond, but with blue eyes—like Luca's. He had shown a real interest and talent for running the exclusive champagne empire. Yet, his father had left the estate to him. Not Marcel. Did that mean he wanted Luca to run it? That he'd forgiven Luca for his mother's death?

Something tightened in his chest.

His father had died before Luca had the chance to ask if he'd forgiven him. He'd also died before telling Luca about Marcel. Had he wanted Marcel to inherit and run the Legrand estate?

Luca revved the engine.

He'd never know what his father wanted, but whatever it was, it didn't change the fact that what Marcel was doing was shitty. He'd almost confided his suspicions to François but decided against it. Since his mother's death, Luca had always taken care of his affairs himself. This was no different, and if he was right, if Marcel was manufacturing these "incidents"—which only required an anonymous call to a tabloid divulging Luca's whereabouts, readily available on Google Calendar—then Luca would figure out a way to take care of Marcel himself.

The first step was to take a hiatus from his high-profile life, making sure no one would know where he was. So he'd rented a flat in a quiet part of town through a discreet agency, he'd started growing a beard—which itched like mad—and he'd been driving his Ducati around Paris. No one would suspect Luca Legrand, professional driver, to be on a Ducati, a make driven by an opposing team. He'd even bought himself a new phone with a new number so he wouldn't be contacted by friends…or tracked by Anika.

Only one problem.

He was bored stiff and had no idea if this hiatus would help with the mess he'd created.

No. The mess Marcel has created.

Grinding his teeth, Luca revved the engine again, released the clutch and sprang forward just as the light changed to green. The thing was, before he'd known who Marcel was, he'd liked him. The man was smart, competent and had seemed like Luca's only ally when every other employee of the Legrand estate—*they aren't employees, they're family*, his father had always said—had shown him little more than polite but cold deference. Something else his father had always said was that trust takes time. Then there was forgiveness...

Luca took the next corner hard and when he spotted a police car at the other end of the street, he reminded himself to slow down. "You don't need to break any more fucking laws," he muttered to himself.

Just to be safe, he turned down a narrow side street—the kind that drove tourists crazy because they went unmarked on tourist maps—and then turned down another, which was narrow and deserted.

No, it wasn't deserted; there was a motorcycle—a Honda Shadow—parked at the side of the road beside an antique shop. The man astride it glanced Luca's way, watching him as Luca drove past. At the corner, Luca checked his rearview mirror.

Something was off. He could feel it by the way the man's helmeted head followed his departure. After Luca turned the corner, he stopped the bike by an empty storefront and parked. Leaving his helmet with the shaded visor on, he walked back to the corner and peered down the street.

The man was in the process of pulling off his helmet, and under that he wore a balaclava. With a final surreptitious glance up and down the street, the man strode into the shop with a crowbar hanging from his fingertips.

Fuck.

It was just his luck.

Luca's one goal was to avoid trouble and here he'd stumbled across a robbery in the middle of the goddamn day.

For the first time in two days, Jasmine forgot everything that had happened and wandered with delight through the shop she'd found using Google maps. It was off the beaten track, down some lonely little cobblestone street. And it was full of treasures.

This was not the type of pawnshop she was familiar with from the United States—a seedy place with bars on the windows where a greasy man wearing an undershirt picked his teeth behind an enclosed counter. This was a delightful boutique with beautiful items carefully displayed, everything from lamps and pots to clothing and jewelry.

"This is so…Paris," she said quietly to herself as she gazed about the tiny space.

There were so many exquisite pieces in the shop to choose from: necklaces, bracelets, earrings. There were also hand-embroidered silk scarves, funky original hats and handbags. There were antiques and what had to be one-of-a-kind items, like the silver oil lamp that reminded her of the stories Auntie Bibi used to whisper at bedtime when she slept over at her cousins as a young girl. Adventures and genies from *Arabian Nights*. She picked up the lamp, considering. Maybe this lamp was a sign that she should have her own adventure, just like Ash encouraged.

Though, a sex-venture?

Jazz smiled to herself. Crazy.

"Est-ce que je peux vous aider?" the man behind the counter asked.

"I'm sorry," Jasmine said, making her way toward him, the lamp, a silk scarf and a necklace clutched in her hands. Not that she needed any of the items but the prices were so good and Jazz was a sucker for a good deal. "I don't speak French. Do you speak English?" She leaned on the display case, her gaze drawn to the gorgeous jewelry inside.

"Yes, a little."

"Those are so pretty," she said, pointing to a pair of emerald-drop earrings.

"Would you like to take a look?"

Oh, yes please, she nearly gushed before she remembered her reason for being there. She absently rubbed the polished silver of the lamp and said, "I have a ring I'd like to sell."

"To sell? May I see?"

She set the lamp down on the counter and reached into her purse. Room key. Wallet. Cell phone. Passport. Hmm...where had she put that ring?

"It's in here somewhere." She dug around. Seriously, where the hell was the ring and what would she do if she'd lost it? She was sure Parker had paid about twenty grand for it. Not that she'd looked it up online or anything.

Okay. Maybe she had.

She located the ring at the bottom of her bag and placed it on the counter for the man to inspect, straightening her shoulders as he picked it up and scrutinized it through the lens of a loupe.

"C'est belle," the man murmured as he checked the ring from all angles.

The bells over the door tinkled but she didn't bother to look because something inside of her had shifted. An unknown weight lifted from Jasmine's shoulders, making her feel like a brand-new person. Could she really put her broken engagement behind her and be the woman Ash had described—carefree and adventurous? A woman who lived in the moment and was on the lookout for a sex-venture…

"Mettez-vous par terre!" a deep male voice shouted.

She turned toward the voice but nothing about the man behind her made sense. It was like she'd stumbled upon the set of a movie and her already muddled brain was having a hard time computing why a man would be wearing a ski mask in spring and brandishing a crowbar.

To her bewilderment, he strode forward and smashed the display case she'd been leaning on with one massive blow.

What the…?

"Écoutez-moi!" He shouted right in her face.

So weird. Was she dreaming? Because this whole thing had an otherworldly quality to it and it just got worse when the dude reached into his beat-up jacket, pulled out a gun and pointed it at her.

"Par terre!"

Before Jasmine had time to consider what the man

was shouting, he grasped the back of her neck and shoved her to the floor.

Oomph!

That hurt.

But now that she was on the ground, the thief ignored her and she lifted her head to find him swiping handfuls of jewelry and dumping the items into a leather satchel. Her ring was among the things he took.

Something inside of her gut, something hot and heavy and furious, was not about to lie benignly on the floor while some petty criminal robbed this delightful shop.

And her.

After all she'd been through? She deserved that fucking ring. Or, rather, she deserved the money from that fucking ring so she could move on from the disaster that was her life.

With energy she had no idea she possessed, Jasmine sprang to her feet, grabbed the outstretched arm of the thug and clung to it like her life depended on it.

"You fucker!" Jasmine growled, twisting his arm in a move she'd learned in a self-defense class, forcing the man to drop the gun. She grabbed the strap of the satchel, pulling it off his shoulder.

"Salope!" The man swung the crowbar catching the side of her head.

The pain in her temple was so sharp and stinging, that warrior-Jasmine drained out of her system as she curled on the ground, gripping the satchel like a beloved teddy bear, feeling like she might vomit from the pain. What happened next would have confused her at the best of times, but her head was still spinning from being clocked and her body was still pumping with adrenaline, lack of sleep and jet leg...

There was a crash.

Followed by a wet *thunk* and a man cried out in pain.

A body crumpled heavily half on, half off her.

A hand appeared in front of her face, gesturing for her to take it in order to help her to her feet. *"Ça va?"*

And then Jasmine was standing on noodle-y legs, gazing into the face of a stranger. The man wore a black leather jacket and a black helmet with the visor raised, revealing a face with a scruffy beard, dark brows and...the clearest, bluest, most amazing eyes she'd ever seen.

And then there were four eyes, then six...

"Mademoiselle?" He snapped his fingers in front of her face.

She shook her head, and then wished she hadn't as stars appeared, dancing in front of her open eyes. She would have fallen if not for the strong hands gripping her arms, holding her up.

However, there were equally strong hands tugging on the strap of the satchel she was still clutching. The thug on the floor grappled for the bag and two things happened simultaneously. The bag slipped from her hands, spilling the contents on the tile floor just as a black leather boot swished past her line of vision, kicking the thief in the face and knocking him out. The rest happened in slow motion. Rings, earrings and necklaces scattered, jumping and skittering across the polished tile floor like live things freed from captivity. Jasmine caught sight of her ring bouncing along the hard floor, ricocheting off the bottom corner of the counter and landing—plunk—inside the passing boot of the stranger.

Without thinking, Jasmine lunged for the man's leg, reaching into the top of his boot for her ring, but he shook her off, glaring down at her and speaking harshly—probably cursing—in French. Then the man stilled, his head jerked toward the door and the street and Jasmine became aware of the sound of sirens approaching.

"Merde!"

With one powerful shake, the six-eyed man dislodged Jasmine from his leg and strode toward the door.

"Wait!" Jasmine scrambled to her feet and hurried out after the stranger in black. Once on the street, she saw him jogging toward a corner and Jasmine took off after him, calling, "Please, wait! You've got my ring!"

However, running in high heels was nearly impossible on the cobblestone street, so Jasmine paused to pull off her sling-back sandals and hurl them away—she'd grab them later. Then she ran the rest of the distance in bare feet. Her head pounded like a drummer was between her ears, playing a solo at a heavy metal concert.

When she got to the corner, her legs wobbled and she could barely see straight.

There.

The man with her ring was straddling a motorcycle, the engine roaring to life as she stumbled toward him, stepping onto the road, holding her hand up to stop him.

Her brain must not have been functioning, because just as the man revved the engine of the motorcycle the world went sideways, and where once there was a street, a man and a motorcycle, there were now only quaint French rooftops, an impossibly blue sky and a bird flying at an odd angle.

Then everything went black.

CHAPTER THREE

JESUS FUCKING CHRIST.

Why couldn't Luca mind his own damn business? Not only had he found himself caught in a robbery, the police were only a block away and now a foreign woman—based on the fact she was shouting in English—had fainted right in front of his bike.

"Non. Non, non, non." Luca put the bike in neutral, jumped off and bent down beside the crumpled woman. He shook her shoulder. *"Reveillez-vous." Wake up.*

The woman moaned, her lids fluttered and then she passed out again. He could see the beginnings of a bruise blossoming along her hairline.

"La vache!" The words scraped the back of his throat. Glancing up and down the street, Luca weighed his options. What if he propped her unconscious body in a doorway...

A quick survey of the street revealed that the two closest doors were covered in paper with signs in the window advertising space for rent.

Not good.

The sirens were loud and close.

Dammit. He couldn't leave her. And he definitely

couldn't get caught at the scene of a crime. He'd wind up in another media shitstorm.

Luca fit his hands beneath the woman's arms and lifted her to her feet. She briefly came to, giving him just enough time to instruct her to straddle the bike. However, once she was astride, she slumped forward.

The sound of more sirens approaching from another direction got Luca's pulse racing. He scooted the woman's body forward on the seat—God, she wasn't very big, was she?—and then straddled the seat behind her. He shifted into first and then wrapped his left arm around the woman's waist to hold her steady while he slowly drove the seven blocks, down side streets and alleys, to his rented flat. The ride only took ten minutes and would have been faster if he could have shifted into a higher gear, but that was impossible to do while holding on to an unconscious woman.

The fact she was still out cold was not a good sign.

She better not die.

What the hell was he doing, bringing an unconscious foreigner back to his flat? He must be out of his mind. Luca could see the headlines smeared across the papers and news channels: Dead Foreigner Found in Luca Legrand's Secret Residence. Foul Play Suspected.

But what choice did he have?

Luca parked his motorcycle in the underground lot, carefully scooped the woman up into his arms and carried her to the elevator that would take him to the fifth floor.

Once inside the flat, he laid her on his bed, got an ice pack out of the freezer—one he kept for when his leg ached—wrapped it in a towel and placed it on the woman's temple.

"Ne me quitte pas," he whispered, brushing hair off her forehead and temple so he could press the cold pack against her wound.

"What does that mean?" she asked softly, her eyes still closed.

Oh, thank God. "I'm asking you not to die. Please."

A small smile touched her lips and she covered his hand with hers. Her touch was light and cool, and Luca felt a stirring of tenderness toward this complete stranger.

"Okay," she murmured. "I'll try."

Then she passed out again.

Rubbing his temples, he gazed down at the slight woman who took up less than a third of his bed. She was showing all of the signs of a concussion; he'd seen it too many times to count on the racing circuit, and although he couldn't risk taking her to a hospital or calling an ambulance, he had to get her medical help.

Back in the bedroom, in the drawer of the small bedside table, was his old phone, the one he hadn't turned on in two weeks. He grabbed it, booted it up and typed a name into his contact list. Then he pressed the call button. As the phone rang, his heart beat fiercely in his chest.

It wasn't anxiety, nor was it adrenaline. This was something else, like he was teetering on the edge of a precipice, vertigo pulling at him, forcing him to jump, and just as he felt himself fall...he noticed the rocks below.

Jasmine woke up to the sound of her own groans. She lay there for a few minutes, listening to the pounding cymbals inside her head, each clash punctuated with a sharp pain that lanced the side of her skull and reverberated through her temples down to her jaw.

Random images from the last few days flashed through her brain. Her wedding had been cancelled, she'd boarded a plane to Paris...

Jasmine's stomach heaved dryly as she recalled nearly getting kicked off the plane. But she hadn't, had she? She'd made it to Paris, right?

Then what...?

Hmm...? Why was it so hard to remember? Was she hungover? She sat up and her head swam like she was wearing glasses with the wrong prescription. Wait a second, she didn't wear glasses, did she?

She touched her face. No glasses. Then Jasmine rubbed her eyes, and when her vision cleared, she took in her surroundings. She didn't recognize a thing.

Where the hell was she?

"Ah, our patient is awake."

Jasmine turned her head—too quickly—causing her to squeeze her lids shut in pain. When she opened her eyes, she saw a man she'd never seen before. He was tall and thin, wearing a tailored shirt and pants. His face was all angles with sunken eyes and cheeks that made his cheekbones prominent. He had close-cropped salt-and-pepper hair and smiled kindly.

"Who are you?"

"My name is Hugo Caron. I am a doctor." The man spoke English slowly, with a French accent.

"Where am I?"

"You are in a private residence in Paris."

"In Paris?"

"Yes. You have bumped your head and I believe you

have sustained a concussion. I need to perform some tests to see how serious it is."

When the man stepped to the side of the bed, Jasmine realized there was someone else in the room. Another man who stood in the shadows.

"Who's that?" she asked, pointing.

The doctor turned, as if he also hadn't realized there was someone there. "That is…" he began slowly, "the man who found you. You were unconscious on the street. He brought you here and called me."

"Oh."

Why was everything so foggy? Why did none of this make sense? What had happened to her once she'd arrived in Paris?

"Oh!" She put her hand to her mouth, a snippet of a memory returning.

Have yourself a sex-venture. It was Ashley's voice in her head.

Slowly this time, Jazz took in her surroundings. The queen-sized bed with the dark sheets and comforter. A masculine choice. The room, a foil to the suite at the hotel—oh, wait, she remembered the hotel! It was airy and light and decorated with antiques—this room was painted taupe and had modern furnishings.

"I'm going to do some tests and then ask you some questions, okay?"

Jazz nodded but stopped herself when the motion caused instant nausea. "Okay," she whispered.

The doctor shone a light in each of her eyes and then asked her to follow his finger as he moved it from side to side in front of her face. He checked her ears with a scope, and her hearing by speaking quietly into each one. With gentle fingers, he touched a tender spot on the side of her head.

"Ouch."

"I'm sorry." He tilted her head up and to the side to get a better look at whatever injury she'd sustained and he *hmm*ed.

"Okay. Straighten your arm out to the side," the doctor instructed. "Now I'm going to push down, try to resist. Good." He changed his grip so that he held the underside of her arm and asked her to push down against his hold and then he did the same on the other side.

Following that, he helped her to stand and asked her to balance on one leg and then the other, and each time he instructed her to touch her finger to her nose while balancing on one foot. There were some more balance and coordination tests before he helped her back onto the bed. He pulled up a chair right beside it and leaned forward.

"I'm going to ask you some questions, okay? You might not know the answers to some but don't worry. It's normal to experience some short-term memory loss after a head injury."

"Okay." Jasmine touched the side of her head gingerly.

The doctor proceeded to ask her full name, where she lived, what she did for a living. All of those were easy to answer. She may have fibbed that she was still employed.

"How long have you been in Paris?"

"Just a day. I think. What day is it? The twenty-fifth?"

"Yes, June twenty-fifth. Good. Where are you staying in Paris?"

"Um…a hotel. It's very pretty, very posh."

"Do you remember the name?"

"Ahh…l'hotel…d'something?" Jasmine bit her lip. "I can't remember, but it's near the Eiffel Tower."

The doctor raised a single brow. "I see. So, what brought you to Paris?"

"It's my honeymoon."

The man straightened. "And where is your husband, madame?"

"My husband?" Jasmine put a hand to her forehead. "I'm sorry. No. It's not my honeymoon." She shook her head and then wished she hadn't. "I'm not married. I just always wanted to come to Paris on my honeymoon." The words came out in a flurry.

"So, are you here with anyone?"

"Um…no. Just me. By myself." Jasmine was vaguely aware of the doctor getting up and going to speak quietly to the man who had been observing from the corner of the room.

"What happened to me?" Jasmine asked.

The doctor didn't answer as the conversation between the two men increased in volume. Were they arguing? Over what? Surely not her?

"Excuse me?" She waved. "Hello?"

Still the men did not respond. The doctor was gesturing at her and speaking rapidly in French. The other man made some guttural remarks and then threw his hands in the air.

"Hey," Jasmine called. "Can someone please tell me what's going on?"

"*Oui, bien sûr.*" The doctor turned toward her. "We

were just discussing your situation. You have a mild concussion. It's nothing to worry about. However, you must be observed for twenty-four hours." He glanced back at the man in the corner. "I can take you to the hospital—but you have no passport."

"Oh, yes I do," Jasmine said. "It's in my bag."

"And where is your bag, *mademoiselle*?"

"It's—" She bit her lip. Blinked. "Isn't it here?"

The doctor turned to speak quietly to the other man who answered quickly. "*Non.* You have nothing here except for what you are wearing."

"Really?" Where the hell was her bag? It would have everything. Her phone, her hotel key, her ID, Parker's credit cards!

Dammit!

"So," Jasmine said slowly, "what will happen to me if I go to the hospital?"

"You will be asked to show identification and because you don't have any, they will have to contact the embassy and your next of kin."

Jasmine held up her hand. "No." The last thing she needed was to have to contact her parents, or worse, Parker, and ask for help after being in Paris only one day. She wasn't ready to face him yet. Absolutely not an option.

"What are my other choices?"

"That you stay here. My friend has kindly offered to observe you for twenty-four hours."

The man standing in shadows muttered something beneath his breath. Whatever it was, it didn't sound like he was thrilled with the idea of *observing* her. Well, Jasmine was not overly keen on being watched by a complete stranger, either, thank you very much.

"There must be some other option."

"You don't know where you're staying. You are here alone and have no identification or money. Unless you know someone in Paris, you do not have many choices, *mademoiselle*."

Slowly—very slowly—Jasmine tilted her head to the side. "What about you? Can't I stay with you?" She pointed at the doctor.

"*Je suis désolé*. I'm sorry but it is impossible. My work has me flying to Italy this evening." The doctor turned toward the other man and gestured him forward. "Luca is a good man." The doctor coughed as if to cover up a chuckle. "He will take excellent care of you until you remember where you are staying."

"What if I can't remember?"

"Your memory should return soon. But if it doesn't, I'm sure the two of you can figure things out." The man's lips twisted as if to repress a grin. "Now," he glanced at the watch on his wrist. "I really must go before I miss my flight." He nodded to Jasmine. *"Au revoir, mademoiselle."*

The doctor exited the bedroom and the other man—Luca—followed. Jasmine could hear the two of them continuing their heated discussion outside the door, though it became more muted as they moved farther down the hallway.

She pressed the heels of her hands to her eyelids, willing herself to remember what had happened. Something.

Anything.

But for the life of her, the last thing Jasmine remembered was Ashley saying, *Buy condoms, lots and lots of condoms.*

* * *

"She can't stay here," Luca insisted once the bedroom door was closed.

Hugo, who was the team physician for Luca's racing team, had not only treated Luca after various wipeouts— including the shattered leg that had ended his career— he'd been a close friend ever since Luca joined the team five years ago. While he'd briefly explained his predicament with the family estate, and Hugo understood his need for discretion, Luca had kept most of the details to himself. Including the robbery.

"I'm sure she'll remember the name of her hotel by the morning. Anyway, you know how important observation is in these first twenty-four hours. This woman has no one to watch her." Hugo smiled gently. "Except you."

"Isn't there another way? I am supposed to be lying low. Not harboring an amnesiac tourist."

"It's only for one night."

Luca groaned in defeat.

Hugo patted his arm. "Everything will be fine." Just then, Hugo's phone dinged and he tapped on it. "My cab is here." He tucked his phone into his pocket and headed for the front door.

"Hugo, wait." Luca exhaled. He hated the fact that he had to say this. "You can't breathe a word of this to anyone, do you understand?"

"Of course." The expression Hugo wore was kind. And most welcome after the way others had treated him since the sex scandal. "Give her acetaminophen for the pain. You know the drill. Rest. No TV." Hugo reached for the door handle. *"Bonne chance, mon ami."*

Luca banged his head—once, twice, three times—against the closed door after Hugo left, and then a noise from down the hall had him spinning around. The woman stood there, eyes wide, her feet bare, thick waves of dark hair shadowing half her face.

"I'm sorry."

Her soft apology did more to diffuse Luca's anger than he would have expected. "Why are you sorry?"

"For putting you out." She gestured to his flat in general. "It's obvious you don't want me here." She walked toward him, taking careful steps. Whether it was because her head hurt or because she was scared of him, Luca couldn't tell. "It's just…" She seemed to be weighing her words. "I don't think I could deal with a hospital waiting room or the embassy right now. I'm still feeling a bit dizzy."

Hugo was right…whoever this woman was, she needed to be taken care of. "It's okay," he said eventually, forcing a smile. "I've changed my plans for this evening." *Plans? What plans, Luc?*

"Oh." A little wrinkle formed between her brows.

"Please. You are welcome to stay the night."

"Are you sure?"

"Yes."

She took a tentative step forward and then another until she stood right in front of him. The top of her head came to just below his chin, her face was tilted up so she could meet his gaze. Her lips were pink and full—the kind of lips Anika would have paid a fortune for—but it was her eyes that captivated him. Liquid brown, like melted chocolate, with smudged mascara that rimmed her wide eyes, only making them appear larger.

There was no fucking way he could say no to those eyes.

"My name is Jasmine. Jasmine Sweet." Her lips trembled with an uncertain smile as she extended her hand. "And you are Luca…?"

"Luca. Luca Deschamps," he lied.

CHAPTER FOUR

THE MAN UNNERVED HER.

There was an intensity to those blue eyes—so dramatic against his dark brows, dark hair and olive skin—that made her feel as if his gaze was boring inside of her, seeking something. But what? It left her feeling shaky and…tingly.

Could be the concussion.

Still…somehow, she felt comfortable here. She'd only half lied when she'd told him why she wanted to stay. The truth was, he was doing her a favor. Now she could put off dealing with Parker and her family until later. Plus, it was one thing to be traveling solo when she knew where she was staying. It was another when she was concussed, confused and without any identification.

"Are you hungry?" the man asked.

"What time is it?"

He flipped his wrist to check his watch. "Seven thirty."

As if on cue, her stomach rumbled and she laughed, though it sounded false to her ears. "I guess so."

"Come. Sit."

She followed him into the open-concept kitchen,

dining room and living room. Like the bedroom, the space was stark. Wood floors, a plain gray leather couch, white walls with dark beams overhead and the floor-to-ceiling windows that seemed to be the norm in Paris.

Jasmine sat on a gray leather barstool at the breakfast counter, leaning her elbows on the granite surface, her hand going automatically to her aching temple.

"Un moment." The man—Luca—strode back down the hall, returning a moment later with the ice pack and two tablets. He first placed the pack against his cheek, murmuring something in French before passing it to her. "It's still cold. It'll help with swelling and bruising."

"Thank you."

Then he dropped the tablets into her upturned hand, his fingers accidentally grazing her palm.

There were those damn tingles again.

She frowned, which hurt. Still, her gaze followed him as he opened a small refrigerator, removed a glass jug of clear bubbling liquid, poured it into a tumbler and handed it to her. She took a sip of the sparkling water, which burned quite pleasantly as she swallowed the pills.

"Are you okay to sit? Do you need to lie down?"

"I'm fine, thank you."

His lips turned up at the ends—not a real smile—as he prompted her to apply the ice pack by taking her hand and placing it against her head.

"It will help."

Jasmine closed her eyes as she iced, ignoring the tingles—and certainly not thinking about the source of the tingles. Once again, she willed herself to remember what had happened after her arrival in Paris, but there was nothing behind her lids but blackness interspersed by shards of light that flashed with each beat of her pulse. For some reason, trying to remember made her head hurt more, so instead, she simply listened to Luca work in the kitchen.

Cupboards opened and closed. The sound of a nearby drawer as it was sliding open and closed on its runners. A knife against a cutting board. Slicing. Another drawer and the sound of cutlery. The clink of glass against the granite countertop followed by the pop of a cork and the gurgling of liquid being poured.

When she opened her eyes, a glass of red wine sat in front of her, as did a plate of various cheeses, finely sliced meats, nuts and olives that he'd placed in the middle of the counter between them.

Luca was tipping his own wine glass back and Jasmine noticed the movement of his Adam's apple as he swallowed. He had a strong neck. Lots of tendons and muscles that worked in harmony.

And then he caught her staring. "Yes?"

She cleared her throat and pointed at her glass. "Should I be drinking?"

"Just a glass. It's good for you. But then water." He gestured to the platter of food. "Please."

Hesitantly, Jasmine reached for a piece of cheese. Oh, it was good, and the more she ate, the more hungry she felt.

When was the last time she'd eaten?

Glancing down, she noticed her dirt-smeared blouse. When was the last time she'd changed? Showered? Turning and tilting her chin in a way she hoped was inconspicuous, Jasmine gave her pits a sniff.

Ugh. Not the freshest.

"Um…" Jasmine began after eating a handful of nuts and three slices of meat. "I hate to trouble you, but would I be able to take a shower?"

The man turned from where he'd been pulling items out of the small refrigerator. "It's not a good idea."

"Excuse me?"

"Taking a shower is not recommended. If you faint, you could hurt yourself." He poured flour onto a plate and added spices with his fingers from pinch jars on the counter. After wiping his hands on a nearby towel, he said, "Come with me."

Jasmine eased off the stool onto her bare feet. The act of standing made her light-headed and she kept a hand on the wall as she followed Luca slowly down the hall, right to the end where there was a large bathroom tiled in slate-colored travertine. There was an ultramodern glassed-in shower big enough for two and a large free-standing soaker tub with a washing wand propped at one end.

"Don't fill the tub," Luca said, gesturing to it. "There are towels here." He pulled a thick white towel out of a cupboard. "I'll find some clothes for you and leave them in the bedroom."

"Oh, thank you."

"Dinner should be ready in forty-five minutes."

"Okay."

Jasmine leaned on the counter for support and turned to find blue eyes scrutinizing her, making her already wobbly knees feel weaker.

"Do you need help?"

Jasmine swallowed.

Was he serious? Would he actually help her? She

glanced at his hand propped on the side of the door-frame. Tanned. Nicely shaped fingernails. Big hands.

What would it feel like to have them removing her clothing?

Helping her into the tub?

Washing her body?

Oh, God.

The tingles she'd been feeling all evening spread from her extremities down her lower back and abdomen, culminating at the very juncture of her legs.

"*Mademoiselle*? Are you okay?"

Jasmine realized her breaths were coming in short little pants and she was gripping the counter like a life vest in an ocean of orgasmic waves.

"Fine," she said quickly. "I'm totally fine."

"Do you need my help?" he asked once again.

She met his gaze. There was concern there and nothing more. This man was not coming on to her, as insistent as her imagination was. Luca was simply being helpful. And kind.

She smiled what she hoped was a reassuring smile. "I'm all good."

"*Bien.*" He stepped back out the door. But before he left, he ducked his head inside the bathroom one more time. "*Mademoiselle*? Please, keep the door open."

Luca left the woman in the bathroom and went to the wardrobe in the bedroom. There was very little to choose from that would fit her, as the collection of clothes he'd brought was sparse. In one drawer he found a pair of shorts that could be tightened with a drawstring and one of his favorite T-shirts from the Red Bull Ring MotoGP event in Austria, 2016.

He left the items on the bed and then went to stand outside the door of the bathroom. It was partially open. He raised his hand to knock, but before he did, his glance went to the mirror, visible through the opening.

Jasmine's back was to him—her bare back.

Merde...

Her spine swayed gracefully and there were two delightful little dimples at the top of her buttocks. Her skin was a flawless caramel color, a contrast to the dark hair that cascaded in waves between her shoulder blades. Her ass was...

Jesus, her ass...

Clenching his fists, Luca turned away from the barely opened door. What the hell was he doing? Now he was a fucking voyeur? This woman's mere presence was trouble enough. The last thing he needed to be doing was ogling her through a semiclosed door. He certainly did not need to be entertaining thoughts of running his finger down the indent of her backbone, dipping into one dimple and then the other and cupping the glorious globes of her ass in each of his hands.

Squeezing before exploring...

Enough!

With a strengthened resolve, he knocked on the wall beside the partly open door. *"Mademoiselle?"*

"Yes?" Her voice sounded startled. And hopeful.

What the fuck?

"I've left some clothes for you in the bedroom. I can launder your clothes tonight so they are clean for tomorrow. Just leave them on the bed."

"Oh." Her voice sounded breathless. "Thank you."

Luca marched down the hall without another word. He needed to focus his attention on tasks like preparing the fish for dinner. Unfortunately, his body wasn't exactly cooperating.

It's been a long time, Luca...and that ass...

"*Silencieux!*" he muttered to himself.

There was no way he would get involved with an amnesiac, concussed tourist. Honestly. It was a bad idea all around. No matter how much his libido thought differently.

Twenty minutes later, when the fish was warming in the oven, he glanced down the hall with a hint of worry. Should he check on her? What if she'd ignored his recommendation and had filled the tub with water, then fallen asleep or passed out and drowned.

Shit.

He hurried down the hall and was just about to push open the door when Jasmine came out wearing nothing but a towel. The scent of his own shampoo wafted about her and he was forced to squash the insane desire to bury his nose in her hair and breathe her in.

Before tugging the towel from her body and tasting that warm skin.

"Hi." The woman's eyes were wide and gorgeous, and appeared much more innocent, sans makeup. That should have quieted his libido.

It did not. Quite the opposite.

He purposefully took a step back, tipped his head and said, "Dinner is ready. I hope you like fish."

He didn't wait for a response but simply spun around and made his way back to the kitchen where he poured himself a large glass of wine and drank most of it before Jasmine made her appearance.

Jesus.

If he'd thought she looked good enough to eat wearing nothing but a towel and the scent of his soap, he was mistaken. The sight of her in his too-big clothes was—fuck—an instant and immediate turn-on.

"Whatever it is, it smells wonderful," she said, softly. Shyly.

Seriously, she was killing him.

"It's sole meunière. Very simple. Just fish, lemon, butter and parsley. Oh, and potatoes."

She sat down at the counter and shrugged. "Sounds good to me."

Luca took the plates from the oven and set them on the counter. He slid cutlery across, refilled her water glass and went around the counter to join her on the other side. Ten minutes ago he had been famished. Now, sitting within touching distance of the American woman, Luca's senses were so enraptured by her that his hunger for food was displaced by an even stronger hunger. Her skin was still warm from the bath, so warm he could feel heat radiating off her. With the heat came the scent of his toiletries but somehow feminized when combined with her own natural scent.

Then there were her eyes.

Whenever their gazes met, he found himself captivated by her large brown eyes, as if sinking into them in a wonderful way, like Charlie at the river of chocolate in Willy Wonka's chocolate factory. He wanted to stay there, drinking it in, forever.

It was Jasmine who broke his stare, turning her attention to the food in front of her. She delicately cut off a piece of fish and placed it on her tongue.

"Mmm…my God." She closed her eyes while her fork was still aloft. "That is so good." Opening her eyes, she smiled at him. "That's more than just fish and lemon and parsley."

"*Non*. That's all it is. But everything is fresh, of course."

"Of course." She took another bite. "You French really know how to cook."

Luca grinned. It was a cliché, and yet coming from this woman her remark pleased him. They finished their meal in relative silence—except for the odd sound of orgasmic enjoyment, which was not helping to cool his libido in the least—and once their plates were clean, Luca took them to the sink and washed them.

"Thank you."

He looked up. "You don't need to thank me every five minutes."

"I know but…" She played absently with a strand of hair. "Your kindness means so much…" Her voice caught but she recovered quickly. "Particularly when I'm a complete stranger to you."

"Really, it is nothing."

She exhaled softly. "Can I ask you a question?"

He glanced up. "Of course."

Her fingers strayed to the lump on her head. "Is there anything else you can tell me about how you found me?"

Luca pulled in his lower lip. His new beard felt strange against his mouth. "*Non*. I found you passed out on the road."

"Where?"

"Not far from here. Maybe seven or eight blocks away."

She touched her head. "And I was alone? No bag, no shoes?"

"Yes."

"Was I mugged?"

"Perhaps. I really don't know." *Liar.* But something in his gut told him that the less anyone knew about this whole ordeal, including her, the better. She might be trustworthy, but he didn't know for sure. Jogging her memory might be like opening Pandora's box, unleashing a situation he couldn't handle right now. He'd let her stay the night, then tomorrow morning he'd figure out his next move.

"God, I wish I could remember."

"Mmm." Luca cut some more slices of cheese and added them to the platter from earlier. Not because they needed more cheese or more food, but to give him something to do during this conversation.

"I've tried to remember, but..."

"It's normal." Luca pushed the platter closer to the woman. "To have a lapse in memory. It will return. Sometimes the more you try to concentrate, the harder it is. You need to rest. Tomorrow you will remember and be able to go back to your old life."

"You speak as if from experience."

Luca broke a piece of cheese and ate it, considering his answer. "I have had a concussion before."

"How did you get yours?"

"I—" Luca paused, only for a second "—have ridden motorbikes since I was eight years old. I have had a few accidents." The last of which ended his career. A ninety percent recovery wasn't enough when it was your gear foot.

"Don't you wear a helmet?"

"Of course. Helmets have saved my life. But you can still get a concussion with a helmet."

She tilted her head as she gazed at him. Her brows drew together as if a thought—or a memory—had just come to her.

"What is the last thing you remember?"

Jasmine plucked a piece of cheese from the plate. She had nice hands, her fingers slim and delicate, her nails painted a neutral color.

"I remember flying to Paris. This was supposed to be—" She glanced up. "A girl's trip with my best friend, but she's expecting a baby—unexpectedly—and…"

Luca waited silently for Jasmine to continue.

"Anyway, I decided to come by myself."

"Sometimes traveling alone is the best way." Luca had enjoyed a few trips to Greece on his own. Just to get away from…everything.

Jasmine took a sip of water. And then another. She had one more before finishing. "Anyway, I drank a lot on the flight. And…" She massaged her neck. "I may have drunk a lot in the twenty-four hours before that." She glanced his way. "Not sure I ate a whole lot during that time." She rolled her shoulders and sighed. "I also haven't slept very much. So it's possible my head injury was simply a result of me passing out from exhaustion, hunger or the world's worst hangover. Likely a combination of all three."

"It is possible," he said slowly. "But by the look of the bruise, it was probably more than that." What was wrong with him? Why didn't he simply agree with her, put her to bed and get rid of her in the morning?

Jasmine shrugged. "Maybe. Which would explain my missing bag. And shoes." Her frown deepened. "Shit. What am I going to do?"

"You will have to go to the embassy. Apply for an emergency passport."

"How can I do that when I don't have any identification?"

"What about in your hotel room? Is there anything there? A copy of your passport? Other ID?"

The woman narrowed her eyes as she thought and then slowly shook her head. "I don't think so. Maybe. But…" She laughed awkwardly. "I don't even know where my hotel is."

Luca stood. This conversation wasn't helping. "You said you didn't sleep much."

She nodded.

"You should get some rest. Sleep is important."

"Let me help clean up, first."

"Non, merci." He indicated the hall. "There is a new toothbrush in the drawer in the bathroom. Please."

"Okay." Jasmine stood and Luca could see that her balance was off because she grabbed the countertop. After a pause and a couple of breaths she made her way down the hall to the bathroom, shutting the door this time.

Damn.

No, not damn. What was he thinking?

When he heard the door open a few minutes later, Luca called, "Jasmine?"

"Yes?"

"I will be waking you up throughout the night. To check on you. Please, don't be alarmed."

CHAPTER FIVE

I WILL BE waking you up...to check on you.

There was nothing sexual about that comment. Absolutely nothing. In fact, it was the opposite of sexual; it was merely a statement made by a man who had been forced to take care of a strange American woman he'd found passed out on the street.

So why did she feel turned on?

She stood in the bedroom doorway, staring at the kitchen. Luca stopped working at the sink to glance down the hall, and even from a distance, Jasmine was immobilized by his gaze. After an indeterminate amount of time, he looked away and the spell was broken. Jasmine hurried into the bedroom, pulled the covers back and crawled between the sheets. The cotton was cool and welcoming to her overheated body. The bed was soft, and for the first time in days, Jasmine relaxed.

Even the throbbing pain in her temple had mellowed to a dull ache.

She turned her head and breathed in. The subtle fragrance of Luca's aftershave clung to his pillow. Spicy. Masculine. Delicious. Lying on her side, she stole the other pillow and hugged it, burrowing her nose into

the faint scent. God. What would it be like to have sex
with him? To feel the scruff of his unshaven jaw against
her sensitive skin? His hands—those strong hands—
touching her body? Exploring. Squeezing. Penetrating.

His mouth—oh, yes, she'd sneaked glances at his
mouth during dinner. Full lips. Expressive. The kind
of lips that were made for kissing.

French kissing.

And maybe more.

Weren't French men known for enjoying kissing a
woman…everywhere?

Jasmine rubbed her knees together.

She'd never experienced that.

Apart from some serious groping in high school
with a shy cowboy, Parker had been her first and only.
He had wooed her with romantic dinners and expensive gifts. He'd complimented her all the time, but with
words, never touch. When he'd told her he wanted to
wait until marriage to have sex, Jasmine had put her
foot down and nixed that idea. She'd read an article
in one of Parker's men's magazines about the impor-
tance of being compatible in bed and had even shared
it with him.

The following night they'd had wine with dinner—
lots and lots of wine, now that she thought about it—
and that had been their first time. Her first time, period,
so she hadn't had anything to compare it to.

Well, except her imagination.

But she'd been too uncertain to ask for what she
wanted, at first, and later Parker had been so busy
with work they could never find the time. And he was
so generous about everything else, she didn't want to
pressure him.

But doubts had crept in and she'd started to wonder if she was somehow inadequate.

She rolled onto her back, the pillow lying un-hugged on top of her. How had she not seen what was going on with her ex-fiancé?

Jasmine had found there were only two ways to alleviate her unsatisfied arousal. Masturbation and fantasy.

Highly detailed sexual fantasies.

They had been her form of counting sheep every night after Parker had nodded off.

She wrapped her arms around the pillow on top of her, letting her mind drift, calling up her latest fantasy involving a sexy space crime fighter, an outlaw in an intergalactic universe.

In this reoccurring fantasy, her hero rescues her from an evil alien's harem and whisks her away to a secluded tropical planet on the outskirts of the galaxy. Her outlaw takes it upon himself to teach her to enjoy sex again. He starts slowly, touching her—only touching—every fucking inch of her body until she is moaning with desire. Then he leaves her wanting on a bed made of some super-awesome alien material that heightens a person's sexual desire when they simply lie on top of it. He returns the next day, this time kissing and licking her entire body.

In her mind, everything was crystal clear...

He's lying between her spread legs, his strong hands pushing her thighs wider, his dark hair—almost black—brushing her belly. A firm tongue nudging her clit one way and then the other. When her hips buck, he holds them down, pressing her into the mattress that sends blasts of arousal across the surface of her skin and into the very depths of her body. When next she raises her hips, he lowers his mouth until he's sucking on her most vulnerable parts, her ass in his hands, kissing, licking, sucking until she can't stand it…

Jasmine's hand roved down beneath the sheets. She wasn't even aware of untying the string at the waistband of the shorts until her fingers delved into her wet heat, mimicking the tongue of her fantasy lover.

God.

You like that?

"Yes, oh, yes," Jasmine murmured against the pillow.

You want this?

"Yes." The word was said on a gasp as she rubbed her clit with the pads of her fingers.

*Oh, baby…*another lick, another suck, *You've got the sweetest pussy. I can't get enough…*

Jasmine lifted her hips off the bed as her fingers penetrated her slick channel. The man in her fantasy looked up from what he was doing. Dark hair. Dark brows. A week-old beard. The bluest eyes.

This wasn't the man from her fantasy.

It was Luca.

Her orgasm hit her like a rogue asteroid, knocking her out of orbit, shattering her as she pressed one hand on top of the other between her legs lest she literally explode.

Luca stood outside the door. The woman was moaning. In pain? Should he go in? He put his hand on the doorknob and was about to turn the handle when she cried out.

Then everything went quiet.

That was not good. He didn't want to walk in to find

her passed out. Or worse. He waited a few seconds before knocking.

"Jasmine? Is everything okay?"

"I'm fine," she called in a high-pitched voice.

"*Bien*. I'll wake you around midnight, okay?"

"Yes. Okay. Perfect. That's good. Thank you."

Luca's hands lingered on the door before he moved to the bathroom to wash up. It was early, yet, for him, only nine thirty, but he should try to rest if he was going to rouse the woman every four hours.

"What else do you have to do?" he asked his reflection. "You've got two more weeks to wait before returning to work. You should be glad for the distraction."

Distraction was fine, but this distraction was a little too…distracting.

He dried his face, the image of Jasmine's nakcd back burned into his irises.

"She'll be gone tomorrow," he muttered, then he hung up the towel and turned the light off.

On his way to the living room, he paused outside her door, listening. No more moans. No more sounds. He hoped that meant all was well. He moved past and settled his frame onto the sofa, reaching for the laptop that sat on the coffee table. Like every night for the past week, he navigated the web to the Legrand website.

When Myra Monte took over the estate's publicity, she convinced Luca to auction off one of three remaining bottles of the Legrand Goût des Rubis. The exclusive rosé blend had been commissioned for the marriage of Grace Kelly to Prince Rainier in 1956, and the bottle included a two-carat ruby in its label. While the bottles were meant to be passed down through the family, Luca had readily made the decision to give one up for the auction if it meant he could maintain control of the estate.

Already the international interest from collectors had been a distraction from Luca's dishonor and prompted an uptick in champagne prices.

Luca entered a name into the search engine: Marcel Durand. He'd done the same thing every night for a week. Watching for any new article or item to show up. He creeped his social media pages and watched for any indication of the slimy eel Luca knew him to be. But, he had to admit, the guy knew how to keep his nose clean.

Luca could almost hear François's voice telling him he could learn a thing or two from this young man.

Salaud! Bastard!

"Literally." Luca ground his teeth.

He was just about to type in another search when he noticed something new. An announcement of Marcel's engagement to Lydia Fournier—hmm…the name sounded familiar. Luca must have met her at one of the functions the company had held in the last eleven months. She was blonde and tall, almost as tall as Marcel, who stood beside her in the photo that had been posted in today's paper. Luca skimmed the article, reading that she had been attending university in Madrid. Then he stopped reading.

So, Marcel was living a perfect life. That would end when Luca exposed him for what he was, though he still had no idea how to go about doing it.

Probably because it was difficult to make a move when he was in hiding, rarely going out during the day. Of course, today had been the exception. This morning, he'd gone for a long ride along the Loire River valley. Riding was the only thing that kept him sane.

But instead of sanity, what had he gotten? An American damsel in distress.

The polar opposite of sanity.

Worse, this damsel just happened to have gorgeous, thick hair, soul-melting eyes and the nicest ass he'd ever seen…

Luca pinched the bridge of his nose. He was a sucker for a beautiful woman in need. Wasn't that how he'd met Anika? She'd had too much to drink during a party on a yacht. He'd held her hair while she got sick.

Without thinking about what he was doing—maybe it was a reminder of why not to get involved with the devil that was woman—Luca typed "Luca Legrand scx vidco" into the search engine.

Despite the fact that Luca's team had had the video taken down—and wanted to take legal action against the original site that posted it—it had spent far too long online before he'd become aware of the situation and had it handled. Millions of viewers had seen it.

Merde.

And millions were still talking about it, if the current search results from blogs and gossip sites were any indication. Luca didn't doubt the internet was rife with illegal copies that could still be viewed somewhere. The whole situation was a nightmare—one that felt impossible to contain. Some sadistic need to punish himself had him opening the original copy of the video and hitting the Play button. The video was dark and amateurish—because when he and Anika had made it, it was for their eyes only—but hcr facc was clcarly distinguishable. As was his as he tied her up, spread-eagled, to the bed. An act that took ultimate trust had been corrupted by exposure to the public.

Luca rubbed his forehead before exiting the video. He returned to the search results online and clicked on the first hit, then scrolled to the comments beneath the article. He knew he shouldn't, but he couldn't help himself. More figurative self-flagellation.

What an asshole.

Luca Legrand can tie me up anytime.

Anika deserves better than that sadistic pig.

He should be thrown in jail...

With a growl, he snapped the laptop lid closed, pushed the computer back onto the coffee table, got to his feet and paced the length of the small living room. What his surfing had confirmed for him was that he could not afford another scandal. He needed to get rid of the American woman first thing without her or anyone else finding out about his involvement.

He could drop her at the embassy—but she had no money and no one to vouch for her.

He could take her back to the street where the shop was to see if she would remember anything. Maybe her bag was still at the shop. Or, more likely, it was at the police station.

He opened the French doors onto the small balcony and went to stand at the rail, breathing in the night air, considering his options. The woman's memory was faulty and she didn't know his real name. Even if she tried to describe him to the police, what were the chances they'd find out it was him? He could vacate the flat, go somewhere else, maybe head south of the city to the villa he'd avoided for twelve years. Perhaps if he just dropped her off at the police station and then drove away...

No. The possibility that someone local would see him and recognize him was too much of a gamble. Once again, it was François's voice in his head telling him it was too risky.

He leaned his elbows on the rail and gazed out.

Wait.

He stood up straight.

Maybe he should call François and get him to help. François was as intent on keeping things quiet as Luca was.

That wasn't a bad idea.

Why hadn't he thought to call the lawyer sooner? He'd do it first thing in the morning.

With the decision made, Luca went back inside and settled onto the sofa, his bed for the night. The ride and fresh air this morning had tired him out. Worrying about the woman had taken the last of his energy and he was tired. However, instead of sleep, images of Jasmine's sweetly curved spine appeared behind his closed lids. Why he let his mind wander in that direction, he couldn't say. Maybe because she'd be gone by morning.

Luca saw himself kneeling behind her, hands on either side of her sloped hips, his tongue tracing the indent of her spine at the top of her ass. Circling those delicate dimples, kissing high up on the globes of her cheeks.

Luca?

"Hmm?"

Will you kiss me? Please?

She turned herself around, presenting the front of

herself. There was a silky patch of hair over her mound, so soft and glistening he had to stroke...with his cheek. "Where do you want me to kiss you?" he asked, gazing up at her.

Everywhere.

"It would be my pleasure," he mumbled quietly.

"Luca?"

Luca's eyes popped open. Jasmine was standing above him, gazing down at him with a—smirk?—on her face.

Fuck.

Sitting up quickly, Luca hoped to hide his raging erection from the woman who had caused it because she'd been starring in his fantasy only two seconds ago. "Jasmine?" He cleared his throat. "Are you okay?"

She nodded and then winced. "I'm fine. But I was lying in bed..." For some reason her cheeks turned pink. "And... I..." Her gaze met his. Her eyes sparkled.

Jesus, was she psychic and able to read his mind? Did she know what he'd been fantasizing about?

"I think I remember what happened."

CHAPTER SIX

SHE MUST HAVE woken him up. He'd sat up abruptly and looked startled by her appearance. Whatever he'd been dreaming about, it must have been good, based on the noticeable bulge behind the fly of his designer jeans. God, his girlfriend was one lucky woman, because that was one sizeable erection.

Hmm. Did he have a girlfriend?

Jasmine realized—with a start—that, first of all, she was staring at the man's crotch, and second of all, she really didn't know anything about him, other than that he drove a motorcycle and had had a concussion before.

"So, what do you remember?" he asked, looking as though he might stand but then thinking better of it. Jasmine hid her smile.

Who was she to judge? She'd been lying in bed totally fantasizing about *him*—in glorious detail—when out of nowhere a memory had surfaced. A quaint little shop on a narrow cobblestone street. A lamp. A scarf. And...a thief.

She'd been caught in a robbery.

It took her a few minutes to describe what she recalled while Luca listened carefully. "And what is the last thing you remember?"

"There was this man wearing a ski mask yelling at me in French. I didn't understand and then he pushed me…" Her hand went to her temple. "Or maybe he hit me." She frowned. "I kind of feel like he did both. Anyway, it's foggy, but that's the last thing I remember." She sat down on the edge of the couch.

Luca nodded slowly. "I'm so sorry, Jasmine. The thief must have taken your bag in the robbery."

"Yes. Probably." She rested her elbows on her knees.

Luca stood and went into the kitchen. "Anyway," he called, "I am happy that your memory is returning. Tomorrow, I'll help you figure out the next steps. You should be back in your hotel and back to your regular life in no time."

"Ye-es." Jasmine drew out the one-syllable word.

"Get some rest. Tomorrow will be busy." He gestured for her to return to the bedroom.

But Jasmine didn't want to return to the bedroom. She didn't want to waste what could be her one and only night with this enigmatic Frenchman by sleeping it away in his bed.

Alone.

Not to mention, she didn't want to go back to her hotel. In her mind she had a flash of the suite: the high ceilings, sheer drapes, a wrought-iron balcony—the room only served to remind her of the fact she was not on her honeymoon and that she was in Paris.

Alone.

She eyed Luca from beneath her curtain of hair. What she really wanted to do was to get to know him more.

No, what you really want to do is to ask him to take

*your clothes off—slowly—and do terrible—wonderful—
things to your body.*

"You know," Jasmine said, getting up and going to
sit at the breakfast bar. The act of standing had made
her feel light-headed all evening, but for some reason
this time it didn't. That had to be a good sign, didn't it?
"I don't actually feel that tired. I feel kind of…wired."

"Wired? I don't understand what that means." Luca
poured himself a glass of water.

"It means I feel the opposite of tired. Is that normal,
with a concussion?"

Luca tilted his head to regard her. "No. I don't think
so."

"Hmm. Weird." Jasmine rested her elbows on the
breakfast bar. "So, I gotta ask," she began. "Does your
girlfriend mind that you have a strange woman spending the night in your apartment?"

Luca blinked. "Girlfriend?"

"Yes." She focused on her hands.

"*Non.* I'm not seeing anyone."

Her head snapped up. "Really?"

"Really."

"Huh."

"What is this 'huh'?"

"Nothing. I'm just surprised." With a new boldness,
Jasmine leaned across the breakfast bar, pulled Luca's
sweating glass toward her and drank from the same
spot he had drunk from.

His eyes followed her. "Why?"

"Because." She examined him from the corner of
her eye. It seemed impossible that he was single. He
was…well, what she knew of him was all positive. He
was kind to strangers, for sure. He had the nicest

hands—she couldn't look at them without imagining them on her body. He filled out his clothes in all the right ways—she tilted her head to eye his crotch again. Very nice.

And then there were his eyes.

He had "I'm going to fuck you" eyes.

And she was here to say yes to those eyes.

But Jasmine wasn't ready to say any of that, so instead, she shrugged, turned the glass on the wet spot it had created on the counter and said, "You just seem like a good person."

He made a deep, guttural sound. "You don't know me."

Jasmine glanced up. "Are you saying you're not a good person?"

Luca shook his head and poured himself a second glass of water. When he didn't answer, Jasmine pushed herself to her feet and wandered into the living room, running her hands along the spartan bookshelves, pulling out copies of books—novels?—in French and a guide to Paris in English. She picked up an ornamental bowl made of alabaster and weighed it in her hands before setting it down again and moving on. What quickly became apparent was that there was not one personal item in this space. No photographs. No personal papers or keepsakes. No clutter. It was completely neutral.

She turned to Luca. "Who's apartment is this?"

"It's mine," he said, though it sounded defensive. Even with the sexy French accent.

"No, it's not."

He cleared his throat. "It belongs to a friend of mine. It's mine for now."

Jasmine was just about to ask why he was staying

at a friend's place, when Luca answered the question for her.

"My girlfriend and I broke up six months ago. It wasn't…amicable. I've been staying here since." He turned his back so she couldn't see his expression.

Was he angry? Heartbroken? Something else?

Hmm. Well, he was single and his explanation made sense. Her gaze swept the room once more and she spied his laptop sitting on the coffee table.

"Hey, can I borrow your laptop?" She strode over and flipped it open.

"Attendez!"

Startled, Jasmine jumped back. Luca strode over and snatched the machine off the coffee table before taking it into the kitchen and setting it on the counter facing away from her. He tapped rapidly on the keyboard before using the touchpad, and after a couple minutes, he brought the computer back and set it on the coffee table in front of her, open to a search engine.

Interesting. What was it that he didn't want her to see? Considering someone had been sporting a healthy erection when she'd woken him up, Jasmine could guess. Was it the head wound or just the fact that she was starting to feel like her old self that gave her the courage to blurt, "Were you surfing porn, Luca?"

"Pardon?" He reached into a cupboard overhead and retrieved two clean wine glasses.

She smiled to herself as she leaned forward to check email.

What the hell was her password?

"Porn," she said absently as she typed some random phrase into the field. She glanced up at him. "You do know what porn is, don't you?"

"Of course I know." He had the good grace to look uncomfortable for approximately three seconds and then his lips twitched and a slow smile spread across his face. He poured wine into the glasses he'd gotten out of the cupboard and came to sit beside her on the couch.

With the warmth of his thigh pressed against hers, Jasmine really couldn't think as each password she tried only resulted in an error message. She was so used to logging in automatically from her phone app—when was the last time she'd needed her password?

"And if I was?" Luca asked, so close to her ear it tickled.

She shivered at the pleasant sensation, her hands hovering above the keyboard like they were as frozen as her email account would be if she failed too many more attempts. Jasmine shut the lid of the laptop, the turn of the conversation seeming more important than email at the moment.

She turned to face him. "I guess that's your business."

He handed her a glass. His gaze was as intense as ever, but something had changed. Something subtle. It wasn't like he was searching; it was like he was trying to convey something. Something important. Something fierce.

Whatever it was, her body responded.

Hard.

Her lips parted and her mouth was suddenly dry. She wet her lips, and Luca's searing gaze dropped to her mouth, lingering there. "Should I be ashamed of watching people make love?" His nostrils flared, as if he was a predator, scenting her. His gaze narrowed as it returned to hers, and the quirk of his lips was on the cynical side.

"No." Jasmine shook her head, unable to break eye contact. "I don't think so."

He nodded and drank. When his stare focused elsewhere, Jasmine was able to take a sip of wine herself.

God, it was good. Smooth, like silk slipping down her throat...

"What kind of an American are you, Jasmine Sweet?"

"Huh?"

"There are stereotypes, you know. About Americans."

"I'm sure there are." Americans had plenty of stereotypes about the French, too.

It went both ways.

"So," she said, raising a brow. "Are you going to tell me what they are?"

His nod was almost imperceptible. "There is the puritan American. Someone who thinks the body and bodily functions are dirty."

Jasmine bit her lip.

"Is that you, Ms. Sweet?" He leaned forward.

She held her breath.

"Or..." He backed up and cocked his head to the side. "Are you the kind who enjoys being a woman, physically and sexually, but who pretends she doesn't like sex because she's ashamed of her pleasure?"

The breath that Jasmine finally dragged into her lungs was ragged. When Luca didn't continue, Jasmine asked in a breathy voice, "Are those the *only* stereotypes you have for American women?"

Luca shrugged.

"What about…" Jasmine began. "The American woman who enjoys sex *and* isn't afraid to admit it?"

"Does such a woman exist?"

"Oh, yes." Jasmine set her glass down beside the computer and scooted closer to Luca. "What about the American who likes to try new things?" She reached for his face, wanting—no, needing—to know what his beard felt like against the tips of her fingers. Against her cheek. Her mouth.

As much as Jasmine was willing herself to be this bold, confident sex-venturer, her fingers still shook when she touched him. But she didn't care. And he didn't stop her.

Or turn away.

Or capture her hand and place it firmly in her lap.

No. He simply sat there and let her explore.

His eyes assessed her from beneath lazy lids while she brushed the contours of his face. His beard was both wiry and soft, and under that she felt the strength of his jaw.

In fact, his jaw suddenly hardened as if he was gritting his teeth.

Wasn't that an interesting response?

"What about the American who isn't afraid to ask for what she wants?" Jasmine whispered, her fingers sliding from beard to mouth, tracing the seam and then the top and the bottom lips. Oh, Jasmine was lying her face off right now, but it felt good.

The subtle parting of Luca's lips was an invitation, she was sure of it, and two of her fingers slipped in, just to his teeth and then past. Good lord, his mouth was wet.

And incredibly hot.

Why was he letting her do this? Why was he encouraging her?

Jasmine had no clue; all she knew was that his mouth was completely and utterly seductive, and when he closed his lips around her fingers and gently sucked, Jasmine realized that the simple sensation of suction on fingertips was more erotic than anything she'd experienced.

She pulled her hand from his mouth and without thinking, sucked her fingers into her own mouth, never breaking his heavy-lidded gaze.

"Are you saying *you* are this kind of woman who is not afraid to ask for what she wants?"

With fingers resting against her mouth, Jasmine nodded.

"Tell me, Jasmine. What is it that you want?"

Was there anything more sexy than hearing that question—deep and guttural—from a hot guy with a French accent?

No. There wasn't. Not that Jasmine could think of, anyway.

She dragged her fingers down her bottom lip, past her chin, to her throat. She'd never felt more seductive, more wanton, more womanly. God. If she had only one night to spend with this man who had turned her into a sex fiend with a simple stare and a question, then dammit she was going to make the most of it.

Jasmine wanted to know what it was like to have something this irrational.

Something that would rock her world.

Not only that, she was going to ask for it.

"I want you to fuck me."

* * *

The only reason Luca had been playing along was because he was angry. It was that stupid video—the comments in particular. No one knew the context of that video and he was so tired of being judged for it.

He'd almost longed for her disapproval so that he could unleash some of his angst on her. But she didn't judge. Oh, no. She'd flirted. And then she'd touched him, with a mixture of sensuality and innocence that was so disconcerting Luca found himself caught up in a new game that too closely mimicked his earlier fantasy.

When she'd asked him to fuck her, he nearly lost it.

All of his control was on the cusp of melting away and Luca had to use everything in his power to fight the urge to pull his own too-big T-shirt up over her head and then tug the shorts from her hips. He ground his teeth as an image of him burying his face in her hair and sucking on that tender spot at the base of her neck flashed across his vision.

And that was just to start.

Get a grip, Luca. "I don't think—"

She reached out, took his wine glass from his hand and set it down on the table on the other side of the computer. Then she framed his face with her hands. They were so small and gentle, and they still trembled, which turned him on more than if she was truly this sexual goddess she claimed to be. Her gaze was on his mouth, like she had zeroed in and locked on her target.

"Jasmine—"

Suddenly one of her hands slipped down between them to cover his hand. Jesus. When had he planted his left hand on her bare thigh, trailing his fingers on her supple skin? Luca couldn't remember, but when

Jasmine pushed his hand higher up her bare leg, inching beneath the leg of the shorts, he didn't stop her.

In fact, when she got up on one knee, suddenly giving his hand easy access to the silky skin that stretched up her inner thigh, Luca completely forgot about stopping.

How could skin be so fucking soft?

His hand inched higher and he knew—just knew—her pussy would be bare. The damp heat that was only centimeters from the tips of his fingers teased him, like a wet whisper, asking him to touch. When Jasmine swung her leg over his in order to straddle him, his fingers found the taut cord that marked the juncture of her thigh and pelvis.

God. Her body was so close. So alluring.

He wanted her.

But somehow he refrained from taking what he wanted, from playing with the soft skin of her labia before plunging his fingers deep inside.

She finally settled herself in his lap and Luca groaned because the heat of her body was scorching, even through the cotton of her shorts and his jeans.

"Please…" she whispered against his lips.

It was his fucking fantasy come to life, and yet Luca needed to stop it.

Her mouth was on his, pressed against his, kissing softly as she made little sounds at the back of her throat.

If you don't stop now, you won't.

"Jasmine," he whispered in between kisses. "We can't."

"Why?"

"Because."

"Because, why?"

Oh, Jesus.

Luca gave up. He threaded his fingers through Jasmine's lush hair and held her hard so he could kiss her properly. Her mouth tasted of wine and honey, and he sucked her sweet nectar both voraciously and with care, like he was a ravenous bear and she an unpredictable beehive. She reacted to his kiss by digging her fingernails into his shoulders, all the while rubbing herself against the fly of his jeans. All he'd have to do was pop his fly and slide the legs of the shorts to the side, and he'd be able to bury himself inside of her.

She'd be wet.

And hot.

And probably fucking tight.

God, he wanted her tight little pussy. His cock ached with need, and as she ground down into him, he held her hips and thrust his toward her.

Non!

This could not happen, no matter how much her sweet little pants and gyrating hips made his cock feel like it was going to explode. It was exactly these thoughtless encounters that got him into trouble. He had to stop. Now. Before it was too late.

"Jasmine." He held her hips still and turned his face away. "We can't do this."

She blinked. "Why? I'm single. You're single." Her breath was coming fast from arousal. "There's no reason to stop."

"Yes. There is." Luca searched her face, and when he saw the bruise on her temple he realized he had his excuse. "You should not be exerting yourself, physically."

She touched her head and frowned.

"Hugo made me promise. Believe me, I would like nothing more than to continue this—" He indicated the space between them. "But I am worried about your well-being."

Her lower lip trembled and then hardened. "I see." She sat for a moment, her face turned away, though he saw how she wiped her cheek.

Oh, God. She wasn't crying, was she? He hadn't meant to make her cry. "I'm sorry."

"It's okay," she said, still turned away. "I should probably go to bed."

"Yes."

She drew in a long, shaky breath before climbing off his lap. She still hadn't looked at him. "Good night, Luca."

"Jasmine?"

She stopped and slowly turned. There were no tears on her cheeks, they were simply red. From embarrassment? Luca didn't know which was worse, making her cry or embarrassing her. "Sleep well."

She nodded and then walked quietly back down the hall. The sound of the door closing only made his balls ache more than they already did. A beautiful woman who had no idea who he was, who was willing to go to bed with him? And he'd refused?

Was he out of his mind?

Or was he really changing for the better?

CHAPTER SEVEN

JASMINE WOKE THE next morning with a headache and a sense of remorse. The headache was explainable, but the remorse was confusing, because last night she'd experienced the best kiss of her life.

And then Luca had pushed her away, and all her feelings of inadequacy around sex resurfaced. Even when he'd woken her up in the middle of the night, he had been clinical. Making sure she knew where she was before leaving her alone again.

She sat up in bed, rubbed her eyes and gingerly touched her temple. There was still a tender lump on the side of her head.

Lovely.

Flipping back the covers, she swung her legs over the side of the bed. On a chair next to the wall was a pile of clothes. Her clothes. All laundered and folded.

Seriously?

Not only was Luca a good caretaker, a good cook and super-D-duper hot, he did laundry? And folded it? The man was a catch.

She picked up the clothes and made her way out to the hallway. Just as she was about to turn the knob on the bathroom door, it opened and Luca stood there surrounded by clouds of steam, the masculine scent of expensive aftershave wafting about him while he wore nothing but a towel around his waist.

Low on his waist.

She stared as she hugged the clothes to her chest lest she give into her base urges and reach out to touch him.

His chest—lickably bare—was ripped. Hard pecs covered in lovely dark hair that only added to his masculinity. His abdomen was mostly hairless, which allowed her to count the ridges. An eight pack? Was that even possible? Apparently. And from his navel a line of hair drew a dark course leading down to what promised to be dark pleasures.

Jasmine's mouth watered and her fingers twitched with need.

"Good morning," he said.

"Uh-huh." She couldn't tear her gaze away.

"Jasmine?"

"Hmm?"

He snapped his fingers in front of her face.

Jasmine gave her head a shake and glanced up. "Yes?"

If she thought his eyes had said "I want to fuck you" last night, she read a whole new message this morning. They shone with such an immoral light it was as if they were now saying, "Here's what I'm going to do to you. I'm going to tie you up, have my way with you and only after you've come five times will I fuck you."

Of course, that could have been her imagination.

Was there time for her to have five orgasms before she had to leave? Hell, she'd settle for one…

"I phoned my friend an hour ago. He will be here to pick you up at 9:00 a.m."

"Huh?"

"My friend François. He'll take you to the embassy so you can apply for an emergency passport. I'm sure they'll help you contact your family so they can wire money and you can continue your vacation."

"Oh."

It was as if he'd poked her with a pin, deflating her.

He motioned her into the bathroom and then went into the bedroom and closed the door. The sound of the door locking was not the same as the high-pitched wheezing of a deflating balloon, but it may as well have been because that was how it made her feel.

"Well, there goes my chance for good sex," she said beneath her breath as she closed the bathroom door.

She showered slowly, letting the scent of Luca's shampoo and soap encompass her. "I'll never wash again," she said to herself as she brought a handful of suds to her face to sniff. Wanting to remember this scent forever.

You know how pathetic you sound? Her inner critic asked.

"Yes."

Her ride to the embassy was going to be here in an hour, which gave her no time to enact any sort of seduction plan. But the worst part was, once she arrived at the embassy, she would have to suck it up and call Parker. He was the one who had all of her documentation. Copies of her passport, her birth certificate and driver's license—all of it was in the desk drawer in the living room.

She turned and let the strong spray hit her directly in the face.

Fuck that. There was no way in hell her first conversation with him since their breakup would be one where she had to ask Parker for help. She needed to find a way around that.

Jasmine turned off the shower and dried herself. Getting ready didn't take long when she didn't have any toiletries besides a toothbrush and a men's comb that didn't even make it through her hair. Without foundation, she was unable to cover up the discoloration at the side of her face.

At least her clothes were clean.

And her panties—which were folded very nicely.

Luca folded my panties. And my bra.

It seemed like such an intimate thing to do.

"Enough," she said to herself. "You have got to get this fantasy under control. It's not happening, Jazz. So just stop."

After running her fingers through her damp hair, Jasmine finished dressing and padded barefoot down the hall to find Luca in the kitchen making breakfast.

The first thing she noticed was the wonderfully rich smell of coffee that had a hint of melted dark chocolate. So decadent. On a plate was a baguette cut in half along with a pot of butter and preserves. There was also a plate of eggs and two glasses of orange juice.

"Thank you," Jasmine said, as she stood in the kitchen entry.

Luca nodded and then glanced at her bare feet. "You need shoes."

Jasmine glanced down at her ruby-red toenail polish. "Yes, I suppose I do." She must've lost them along with her purse.

"I'll tell François to take you to a shop first."

"I don't have money."

"He'll buy you a pair."

Jasmine went around to the breakfast bar and sat. "François must be a very good friend."

Luca made a face. She couldn't tell if it had a positive or negative expression. "I've known him all my life."

Jasmine had hoped that Luca would at least join her for breakfast, but he'd obviously already eaten because he was in the process of washing his plate. Once it was set in the rack over the sink to dry, he refilled his espresso cup and took it down the hall to his bedroom.

This really was it. Her sex-venture was over before it had even begun. Such a shame. Watching the clock over the stove like she was an inmate on death row eating her final meal as she awaited the appointed hour, Jasmine decided she would call her parents first, once she got to the embassy. They could contact Parker if need be. Once she had travel documents, she'd change her flight and go home.

What had she been thinking, coming here by herself? She wasn't an adventurer, and certainly not a sex-venturer. This whole thing had been one big mistake. Running away from a situation she didn't want to face was never a good decision.

Just as she finished the last bite of baguette, a telephone rang. Luca strode back down the hall to retrieve it. He checked the screen and said, "It's François."

Her stomach sank. If she looked down, Jasmine was sure she'd find it flopping around on the hardwood floor. With a sigh, she carried her dishes to the sink to wash. However, before she'd finished wiping her plate, she noticed the volume and tone of Luca's voice, and she stopped what she was doing to listen.

Something was wrong.

While she didn't understand the French language, she understood *body* language and Luca's said one thing. He was angry. He paced the room while gesturing wildly with his free hand. His voice was deep and guttural and he spoke so rapidly his words sounded like machine-gun fire.

"Non. Je ne peux pas le croire."

That did not sound good. Jasmine leaned her elbows on the counter as she watched the exchange with great interest.

Luca opened the sliding doors off the living room to the balcony and peered down at the street below. Something was going on because Jasmine heard the cacophony of a crowd even from where she stood.

"Non, non, non, non," Luca said, slamming the doors shut.

Okay, she understood that. It was a lot of no's. Definitely indicating something was making Luca unhappy.

When Luca finally hung up, he slammed the phone against the counter, which surprisingly did not break it, and growled like a caged beast before pacing some more. His head was down and he gripped his hair as he moved back and forth across the small space.

Finally he stopped, turned to her and said, "Okay. Change of plans." He marched to the wardrobe in the front hall and came back with two helmets, two leather jackets and a leather bag. "Put this on," he said, shoving a helmet and jacket at her. "We leave in five minutes."

Jasmine stood barefoot at the front door, stunned by this change in events. Luca stomped down the hall muttering angrily and returned moments later stuffing clothes into a leather satchel and slinging the strap

over his shoulder. Then he donned his helmet, took
her hand and dragged her out the door and down to
the parking garage.

When he started up his bike, she stood beside him
with her visor raised and said, "I thought I wasn't supposed to ride."

"You're fine. Now get on and wrap your arms
around my waist." He flipped down the passenger foot
pegs and waited.

As soon as she'd done as he asked, he put the bike
into first, opened the garage door and ripped up the
ramp and onto the street, narrowly missing a van and
then another one before skirting a group of people that
were milling about between the vehicles, toting micro-
phones and cameras.

What the hell was going on?

"Hold on tight," he called over his shoulder as he
changed gears and wove between cars as he headed
for a main street.

Jasmine leaned against his back, her toes curling
painfully around the teeth on the metal pegs as she
watched Paris slip by at high speed.

Holy shit! Was that the Louvre? She'd seen so
many pictures of the palatial landmark, but now, as
they roared by the building, weaving in and out of the
tourist traffic, it seemed surreal. But the building and
crowds were gone before she'd had a chance to really
take it in, then Luca turned onto a street that paral-
leled the Seine.

"Oh, my God," she whispered to herself a few minutes later. With hands gripping the leather waist of Luca's
jacket, she sat up so she could get a better view. They
were on the other side of the river from Notre Dame Ca-

thedral. The central spire, the ornate stonework, it was such an impressive, distinctive Gothic structure, and even though she'd seen hundreds of pictures of it, seeing it in person took Jasmine's breath away.

So did the speed at which they were traveling.

Luca drove like a madman, changing lanes at speeds that were certainly illegal and highly unsafe.

She'd never felt more thrilled in her life.

When a car driving in the opposite direction turned on its lights and siren, and then spun around to pursue them, Jasmine felt something else she'd never experienced. A tingling at the base of her spine that spread out across her lower back and into her abdomen.

"Hold on," Luca commanded for the third time.

She leaned into him and closed her eyes. This could very well be the last day of her life and if it was…she didn't care.

She was having an adventure!

How the hell had the fucking paparazzi found him? Luca had no idea. François said they were out in full force at the front of the building milling about, waiting for him to emerge. Did they know he was in the company of a concussed, shoeless American woman?

He hadn't had time to think about who might have leaked his whereabouts, he'd been too busy driving and trying to get the hell out of Paris. His adrenaline had kicked in, causing him to drive like he would in a race. It was the best fucking feeling in the world—next to an orgasm, of course—because it was the closest thing to flying that you could get while still staying on the ground. Time moved differently, like breaking speed

limits actually broke the veil of physics and hurtled
him from the laws of this world into the next.

It was a spiritual experience.

So when the police siren had started up behind him,
Luca barely noticed or cared, other than realizing he'd
never be able to take Jasmine directly to the embassy
while the police were on his tail. He'd taken the corner onto Boulevard Périphérique so tightly an ama-
teur would have spun out, and Jasmine had screamed
behind him, burying her hands in his pockets as she
mashed herself against him.

He continued speeding along Périph, headed toward
the A6 that would take him south of Paris. It wasn't
until he was on the A6, the police lost somewhere in
traffic, that Luca had had time to think about who
might have exposed him—once more—to the press.
Had Hugo said something to someone?

No, his friend wouldn't do that.

Who else could have known? Had Anika had him
followed? What about Marcel? Maybe Marcel had
overheard his conversation with François and alerted
the press. Or had Jasmine told someone when she used
his computer last night?

He pulled the clutch and changed gears, rage feed-
ing his need to push the bike to its limits. There was
only one problem; something in his boot, a rock or
something, was driving him crazy. He'd noticed it as
soon as he'd put his boots on but hadn't had time to
stop and shake it out. He wouldn't be stopping, either,
not until he got to Nemours, where he planned to drop
Jasmine off at a train station before he traveled another
hour south to his final destination in the Loire Valley.

By the time he turned off the highway onto D403

into Nemours, the rock in his boot was a constant annoyance, also reminding him that Jasmine was still shoeless. After an hour on the bike, her feet would be getting sore from the metal pegs. He needed to find a shoe store.

Once turning onto the Rue d'Paris, he saw a little shop on the corner and pulled the bike over. He flipped up his shaded visor and turned in the seat. "You see that store, Chaussures Sigal? It will have shoes." Opening up the flap on his bag, he found his wallet and peeled three one-hundred-euro notes from a stack just as Jasmine dismounted and pulled off her helmet.

Her eyes were saucer shaped as she took in the bills. He thought she was going to comment, but she didn't. She snatched the money out of his hand and padded barefoot into the store. That gave Luca time to take off his boot and shake the rock out of it.

Except it wasn't a rock.

No, that wasn't true. It *was* a rock, a *big* fucking rock. Luca picked the ring up off the road and inspected it. The band was small and platinum, made for a delicate finger. The diamond was…huge. Three, maybe four carats. This was an expensive engagement ring.

"Jesus," he muttered to himself. Was it Jasmine's ring? Was that why she'd been chasing him yesterday on the street? Had the ring somehow gotten lodged in his boot during the chaos of the robbery?

What was he supposed to do with it now?

Tell her? But then she would know that he'd been in the store, seen what happened and lied to her. No. He couldn't tell her, but he did have to give it back to her.

Somehow.

If it was hers.

But if it *was* hers, what did that mean? Was she engaged? Where was her fiancé? What the hell was she doing with him?

Luca tucked the ring into his wallet—maybe he'd slip it into her pocket while saying goodbye at the train station. If it wasn't hers…oh, well. Twenty minutes later, Jasmine emerged from the store wearing a pair of sandals and holding another bag in her hand.

She held the bag aloft and said, "I borrowed some money to buy some clothes, too—I got great prices on two pairs of shoes, a blouse, a skirt *and* a dress." She smiled wide, showing her teeth. "I hope that's okay."

"Of course." He swung his head to indicate the seat behind him. "Get on."

"I'm a very good shopper," she continued, as if he'd commented about it. Which he hadn't.

"Great. Now, get on."

"Yeah. I don't think so."

"Excuse me?"

"I'm not getting on until you tell me where we're going, why you're driving like a maniac…" She eyed the bag he had slung across his chest. "And why you have an enormous wad of cash in your wallet."

Dammit. He had no intention of answering any of those questions. Well, he could answer the first one. "*We* aren't going anywhere. I am dropping *you* off at the train station and you are returning to Paris."

She set the bag down, crossed her arms over her chest and said, "No."

"No?"

"I'm not going back to Paris."

"Yes, you are."

She shook her head. "Nope. And I'm not getting on the bike, so…"

"Fine." Luca pulled his wallet out of the bag again and peeled off a few more notes. He held them out to her. "You've got shoes now. You can walk to the train station." When she didn't take the money he leaned over, picked up the shopping bag and dropped the notes inside.

She glanced down at the money and then said, "You know what I think?"

"*Non*. I don't."

"I think you're on the run from the police." Her eyes lit up. "And I think you're worried that I'll turn you in."

If she thought he was some criminal on the lam, why the hell were her eyes so bright and her cheeks so pink? It was like the notion turned her on.

And—bam—like that, *he* was turned on.

Fuck. He had to get rid of her. Quick. She was a liability. "An interesting hypothesis." He pointed to the end of the street. "Take this street across the river and then turn right. The train station is maybe five hundred meters north."

Jasmine's lips twitched. "So, you're saying I need to walk right past that official-looking building on the other side of the street?" She pointed. "Because that's the police station." She smiled. Wide. "I asked the girl in the store. She pointed it out to me."

Oh, for fuck's sake. Luca started the engine and lowered his visor, ready to call her bluff. "*Au revoir*, Jasmine. *Bonne chance*." He was just about to drive away when he remembered something.

He still had her ring.

CHAPTER EIGHT

FOR A SECOND, Jasmine thought she'd been wrong about Luca, that he didn't care about the police and might actually drive away.

Except he didn't.

Oh, he revved the engine like he *wanted* to drive away. He even put the bike into gear. But after some muffled sounds that Jasmine was certain were a string of curse words, he lifted his visor and said, "What do you want from me?"

Jasmine glanced up and down the street. There was no way she could articulate *exactly* what she wanted from this man. Half of the things were illegal—maybe only in Alabama, but still. "I want to come with you." She wet her lips. "Wherever it is that you're going." She had no idea where he was going but she was pretty sure it wasn't back to Paris. And if he wasn't going back, either was she, but for very different reasons.

She blinked as a random imaged popped into her brain...

Luca standing bare chested before his shower, only this time he invited her to join him...

He cut the engine. "Why? Why don't you want to

go back to Paris and continue your nice holiday? Why would you want to come with me? You don't know me."

How could she answer that without sounding ridiculous? She wanted to stay with him because when she was with him, her senses were heightened. Colors were brighter, food tasted better and nothing was predictable. He was the first man to make her feel alive. She knew it wasn't a forever thing, but that wasn't what she wanted. She wanted to experience more of how Luca made her feel.

Electric. Sensual. Feminine.

He was exactly what she needed at this juncture of her life. He was the key to her getting over the disaster of her engagement.

He was what she needed to move on.

But of course she couldn't tell him any of that. So she told another equally true story. "The person who has all the papers and documents I need for a passport is not someone I'm keen to speak to right now." She didn't even have to pretend. The excitement and thrill of the motorcycle ride evaporated instantaneously at the thought of talking to Parker. For the first time in over an hour, the lump on the side of her head throbbed like someone had shoved a knife into her temple. Once the pain abated, she said softly, "I know I have to, at some point, but not yet. I'm not ready."

Reaching down into the bag, she fished out the notes and tried pass them back to Luca. "Please. I promise I won't cause any problems. Let me come with you, just for a few days."

He tilted his head to one side, his blue eyes so much bluer in the sun. She could see the wheels turning and a spark of hope filled her when he exhaled heavily and took the proffered notes from her hand. *"Bien."*

"Does that mean good?" She kind of recognized that word, but the way Luca said it made it sound like it was anything but good.

"It means fine. Come with me. For now."

Jasmine fought the urge to clap and jump up and down. She had to play it cool. She had to show him that he was making the right decision by taking her with him—and she was going to make sure she paid him back.

In whatever way possible.

Preferably on her back.

Or on her knees in front of him.

Perhaps on her hands and knees with him behind her.

Oh, God…

Jasmine climbed onto the back of the bike, her clit throbbing against the leather seat as she snugged herself up against him, the bag of clothes squished between their bodies as she shoved her hands into his pockets.

Yes.

This felt good. It felt right.

"So, where are we going?" she called.

"You'll see."

Without another word, Luca took off, doing a U-turn in the street and heading back the way they'd come in order to merge back onto the highway. While he still drove fast—maybe about ninety miles an hour?—it seemed positively leisurely compared to the earlier frenetic speeds.

The traffic was lighter when they got farther south.

And the countryside? Well, the traditional French land-
scape was like something out of a movie. Rolling hills
of pastureland, vineyards and fields of wildflowers.
On the top of every other hill sat little villages built
out of stone with black tiled roofs, and every so often
she caught sight of a river as the road wound up and
down and around.

But nothing could have prepared her for their destination. Luca turned off the highway heading for one
of the little villages with old stone and brick build-
ings rising crookedly along narrow winding streets.
Luca turned down one street on the outskirts of the
town, and between the trees that lined it she could see
glimpses of the river. The steeply sloping roof of a large
villa rose at the end of the road.

Was that where they were going?

Luca turned down a lane that also had trees on either side. At the end of the lane was what must have
been a twelve-foot-high metal gate, and to the right of
the gate was a humble stone cottage. Luca stopped in
front of the house, turned the bike off and engaged the
kickstand. "Wait here."

He pulled off his helmet and hung it from a handle-
bar, ran his hands through his hair and slowly made
his way to the door. An elderly gentleman opened it,
looked Luca up and down and then gave him a bear
hug.

Was that his father? Had Luca brought her home?

Luca and the man spoke for a few minutes before
the man disappeared and then reappeared with a stout,
elderly woman who practically mauled Luca. She gestured wildly and even from the distance, Jasmine could
tell the woman was inviting Luca inside. He pointed to

where Jasmine was sitting. The man tipped his head in greeting from the door but the woman only seemed to be frowning at her. Luca spoke again and gestured to the house and the man disappeared inside. When he reappeared, he handed something to Luca and, in return, Luca opened his bag and found something that he gave to the man.

What was it? Money?

After one more hug from the woman, Luca jogged back to join her. Considering he had obviously been reunited with people of significance to him, his expression was grim.

What was going on?

She had no time to ask because he popped his helmet back on, and without bothering to do up the strap, he straddled the bike in front of her and started it up. He drove slowly to the gate, climbed off the bike again, took a ring of keys that he'd obviously been given by the man and used one to unlock the gate. He swung it open, came back to drive through, stopped, and then closed and locked the gate behind them.

He mounted the bike again and they drove down the lane until a house came into view.

No. Not a house.

This was a French villa. Or a château or something.

It was a large, whitewashed, two-story structure with a steeply pitched roof of black tiles and vines creeping up the corners.

Luca stopped at the doors of the two-car garage and turned off the bike.

"We're staying here?" Jasmine asked after she pulled off her helmet.

"*Oui.*"

"Who's place is this?"

"It's mine."

"It's yours?" Jasmine asked, aghast.

Shit, he thought. *That slipped out.*

Luca quickly shook his head. "It's mine, just for the season."

"So, who does it belong to?"

Luca should have been planning a story during the drive, but he'd been bombarded by too many memories. Summers here by the river. Rebuilding and riding his motorcycles all over the countryside. That one summer, nearly fifteen years ago, when he and his mother had been returning from town, his mother letting him drive her Aston Martin DB9. The sudden thunderstorm. The dark road. The pools of water.

Driving too fast.

The crash.

"It belongs to an aunt. She's in Switzerland at the moment."

Jasmine studied him as if she wasn't quite satisfied with the story, but she didn't press him as her attention was captivated by the grandeur of the house. The Gauthiers—the elderly couple who lived in the caretaker's cottage—had done a superb job of keeping up the place. Even the ivy wasn't overgrown, considering no one had stayed here for twelve years.

"And she's okay with you staying here now?" she asked over her shoulder as she started to make her way up the gravel path.

"I called her while you were buying clothes," he lied, adding to the lengthening list.

The walk was well groomed, flowers had been

planted in beds edging the walls of the house and the trees were all pruned. Considering what he paid the Gauthiers to maintain the property, he would have been extremely disappointed if things hadn't been kept up. The deal was that the house was supposed to appear lived-in.

It did.

Yet for Luca, the residents were all ghosts.

"And who are the people who live outside the gates?" Jasmine asked as she waited for him to unlock the front door.

"Madame and Monsieur Gauthier. The caretakers."

He recognized the house key among the seven on the ring and unlocked the door.

"They seemed happy to see you."

"I used to come here sometimes as a boy. It's been many years. I'm surprised they remembered me," Luca said quietly as he swung the door open, prepared to be greeted by stale air, dust and spirits.

Instead, the air smelled like lemon and the marble floor shone. Not a speck of dust. His money had been well spent.

"Ho-ly." Jasmine gazed at the sixteen-foot-high ceilings and the curved stairs that led to the second floor. Without being invited, she wandered in through an arched door to the living room, which had the same high ceilings with original beams overhead. The room had an enormous fireplace at one end, and French doors opened up to the terrace out back that stretched the entire length of the home.

The only things that made the house seem uninhabited were the dust covers draped over all the furniture. Luca followed Jasmine from room to room as she explored. It was a one-sided conversation, as she made appreciative comments in each room and he stayed silent. So many memories.

Too many.

After touring the entire main floor—which consisted of the living room, dining room, kitchen, two bedrooms, bathroom and WC—they returned to the front entrance.

"What's up there?" Jasmine asked, pointing up the stairs.

"More bedrooms and bathrooms. But the main floor should be sufficient for our needs."

She bit her lip, and by the way her eyes glowed, he could tell she wanted to investigate further. However, his old room was upstairs and he wasn't in the mood to revisit it.

"Out back there's a pretty park and a pigeon loft that dates back to the seventeenth century, when this was a monastery."

"Are you serious?" Her eyes shone and she took his hand and tugged him toward the door. "Let's go."

Despite the melancholy that Luca had initially felt upon his return, Jasmine's enthusiasm for the estate— a place he had always loved—was contagious. For the rest of the tour, he showed off the property with the pride of someone who had a deep fondness for the place. The large park that led down to the boathouse on the banks of the Loire River. The vineyard to the south, the only part of the estate that was showing neglect. He didn't expect his elderly caretakers to handle that job.

They strolled between the overgrown rows of grapes, and Jasmine stopped. "What kind of grapes are these?"

"Mostly sauvignon blanc, but this vineyard still has some pinot noir vines and some cabernet franc." Luca gazed out over the rows, amazed at how peaceful it was here.

"Why isn't this being cultivated? It seems like such a waste."

"It's a lot of work for...my aunt."

Though Luca could imagine it, suddenly. Cleaning up the rows. Pruning. Weeding. Picking. For the first time since he'd taken over the Legrand estate, the thought of producing wine and champagne seemed more than just a duty, it excited him.

He glanced down at Jasmine, who was watching him with a puzzled expression. "What?"

"Nothing."

They took a path back to the main garden. "You're lucky to be able to stay here. I'm surprised you didn't come here sooner."

"It's a little remote."

"It's gorgeous!"

"You like it here?"

"Are you kidding?" Jasmine's enthusiasm bubbled out as if from a spring. Her cheeks were pink, her eyes sparkled and her hands moved expressively. "This is like a fairy tale." She gazed up at the nearest tree. "What is this? A pear tree? And what's that? Apples? Is this an orchard?"

Luca laughed and then, for the first time that day, he noticed how badly the side of Jasmine's face was bruised. Considering all the excitement of the trip, she hadn't complained once.

"How's your head?" he asked, taking a step closer and reaching out to gently touch her face.

She sucked in a breath. From pain?

"Sorry."

"It's okay," she replied quickly, turning toward him. "I'd actually forgotten about my goose egg."

"Goose egg?"

"Lump on my head." She covered it and winced. "This place could make a girl forget just about anything."

She gazed up at him and everything was forgotten. The paparazzi, the betrayal, the road trip and the ghosts of memories. All Luca could focus on was her.

This petite American woman who gazed at him with a heady combination of longing and lust. Who, despite his distant and questionable behavior, seemed to find his company enjoyable. He reached for her hand and drew her close.

"Jasmine?"

"Yes?" The word was breathy and hopeful. She placed her hand on his chest, and Luca longed to feel her slim hand against his bare flesh. To let her touch him, her trembling fingers exploring him with the same wonder she'd explored the estate.

"Luca?" A male voice called from the terrace.

The spell was broken and Luca's head snapped to attention. Monsieur Gauthier stood up on the terrace, his hand shading his eyes from the sun.

"Ah. Supplies are here. I don't know about you, but I'm starving."

CHAPTER NINE

THE PLACE WAS like something out of a storybook and Jasmine couldn't contain her sense of excitement, excitement that made no sense. Here she was, without a penny to her name, no ID, no passport, stuck on a remote and practically abandoned estate in France with a man who was running from someone, most likely the police.

And yet things had never felt so right.

There must be something wrong with her.

Maybe it was the fact that Luca had almost kissed her in the orchard.

You are getting some tonight! Her inner critic had even traded in her sarcasm for a little bit of excitement.

With a skip to her step, Jasmine followed Luca up to the terrace where the older gentleman waited for them. He spoke rapidly to Luca, pointing inside the house and then gesturing to the grounds. After they finished, the man met her gaze and bobbed his head.

"Bonjour, mademoiselle."

"Bonjour," Jasmine said, liking the feel of the French word on her tongue.

"Monsieur Gauthier, this is Jasmine," Luca introduced them.

In halting English, the man greeted her and welcomed her before turning his attention back to Luca. They ended their conversation with a handshake and the man left by way of a path around the house. When they went back inside, there were three baskets full of staples waiting for them on the kitchen table. Bread, cold meat, cheese, butter, milk, flour, sugar, coffee, and fruit and vegetables that were not in plastic bags but looked like they'd just been pulled fresh from the garden…there was even a box full of pastries.

In addition, stacked in an ironed pile, were freshly laundered linens.

"Why don't you go make up the beds," Luca said, "while I put lunch together?"

Beds? Did Luca say beds?

Oh, hell, no. There were not going to be any "beds" for them. *One* bed. One for both of them. However, that would all be sorted later, so Jasmine took the linens—which smelled like sunshine—to the first bedroom on the main floor. She pulled the dustcover off the queen-sized mattress and got to work. Once she was done, she couldn't help but lie down on top of it. The mattress was a little firm, but that was okay. She gazed up at the high ceilings with the old beams running across. There was a gorgeous antique chandelier above the bed—a little dusty, but still pretty. The bed had one of those old-fashioned canopies arching up from the headboard, which contributed to her sense of being caught up in some modern-day fairy tale. The furniture wasn't buffed to a high polish like the furniture in her hotel, but was nicked and worn, as if well used.

She shut her eyes, and just like last night, images of

Luca filtered through her brain, though with less clarity than her constructed fantasy.

Luca, damp after his shower.

Luca's hard body in front of her as they raced through the streets of Paris.

Luca, smiling seductively with the sun dappling his face through the foliage in the orchard.

Luca kissing her in a way no one had ever kissed her.

Luca…just Luca…

Where had she gone? How long did it take her to make up a couple of beds?

When Jasmine didn't return, Luca went in search of her and found her curled up in the middle of the bed in the master bedroom. Sound asleep.

Instead of closing the door and letting her rest, like he should have, Luca walked softly into the room and sat on the bed beside her. What was it about this woman that compelled him to do such irrational things, like watch her sleep? He'd only known her for twenty-four hours, yet already he felt the need to crawl up beside her and fit her slight body within the circle of his arms and hold her.

Protect her.

Make love to her.

Then do it again and make her scream in ecstasy…

What the fuck is your problem? You barely know her.

Luca got up carefully, so as not to wake her, picked up the rest of the linens and left the room to make up the bed in the room down the hall. After that was done he went back to the kitchen and ate, though his thoughts were still on his unwanted guest.

Unwanted? Really? Or is it that you want her too much?

With a groan, Luca put together another open-faced sandwich with a thick slice of bread, a slab of meat and some creamy cheese, and decided it was time to get busy. He spent the next hour removing dust covers from furniture, testing light bulbs and fixtures to make sure everything was in working order, and then going to check on the hot water boiler. There was an old bag of wood pellets—he had to get some more soon—that he dumped in the burner before lighting the pilot light. Hot water should be ready in thirty minutes. Then he made his way to the garage.

He spent another couple of hours in the garage and in the boathouse, cleaning and checking the old vehicles and boats. After so many hours working in the dust, he returned to the house and headed straight for the bathroom. After cranking the stiff tap and letting the water run through pipes that had grown rusty from disuse, he stuck his hand under the spray to test it. Scaldingly hot. Perfect.

He dropped his clothes and stepped under the spray, rubbing the dust from his skin and hair. There hadn't been room to bring anything other than their toothbrushes and a change of clothes, they'd have to pick up toiletries tomorrow.

How long would she want to stay?

How long did he want her to stay?

Honestly? Luca didn't know. He was completely conflicted over his surprise American guest. His logical side insisted he drive her to Nevers tomorrow so she could catch a train back to Paris.

His physical side?

Luca glanced down, noting the growing evidence of what his physical side wanted. He wanted her naked. On her back. Her legs parted. Her dark hair fanned out on a white pillow. Her lips swollen from having been wrapped around his cock…

He grasped his erection. Jesus, he needed some relief. There was an old cake of soap on a shelf and though it was as hard as a rock, after moistening it, it eventually lathered, giving off a honey and lavender scent. Once he had created some suds in his hand, Luca slid it along his length. He leaned against the tiled wall and shut his eyes, letting his imagination take over as he fisted himself.

Fuck, it had been too long.

"May I?"

Luca's eyes popped open.

He dropped the soap and stood dumbfounded, his erection pointing straight at the object of his desire.

Jasmine stood just inside the curtain—she was stealthy, this one—completely nude. Luca took in her naked body, as if the vision of her could be absorbed through every pore. Her hair, her sultry gaze, her parted lips, her narrow shoulders and full breasts. Her slim waist and curving hips.

Her bare pussy.

He'd known it.

"Would you like me to?"

"To what?" His question came out as a growl.

"To finish." Her gaze dropped to his erect penis. "For you."

Luca fought with himself for all of a nanosecond.

Then she wet her lips, biting down on the bottom one before slowly raising her gaze, a sinful question in her shy smile.

That was it. Battle over.

She had won.

"Yes. Oh, fuck, yes."

But when she grasped the backs of his legs so that she could lower herself to her knees in front of him, her mouth level with his erection while water sluiced down into her upturned face, Luca realized Jasmine hadn't won.

He had.

She'd woken up disorientated. But it hadn't lasted long. Particularly when she'd padded out into the hallway and heard the water running in the bathroom.

Luca was taking a shower.

This was her fantasy. Except she wasn't imagining it; it was happening right here in real time.

Fuck fantasy.

It was time to start living instead of spending so much time wrapped up in her imagination. Without wasting one more second, Jasmine had stripped out of her clothes and left them lying in the hallway. She'd thought for sure Luca would hear her coming into the bathroom so she'd moved straight up to the curtain and pulled it back, only to come face to face with the rawest, sexiest thing she'd ever seen.

Luca was leaning against the wall, naked—a fucking Adonis—with the nicest, hardest cock held firmly in his fist.

Pumping.

She'd blurted, "May I?"

The second Luca had opened his eyes and stood there, all naked and proud, she knew he wouldn't say no.

And he hadn't.

Without even thinking about what she was doing, Jasmine dropped to her knees in front of him and took him in her hands. He groaned at her touch. Groaned. Like what she was doing felt good to him. Like he liked it.

God. It made her feel so...powerful.

Wrapping her fingers around him—sweet Jesus, the man was well proportioned—Jasmine tried to mimic his earlier movements. She must have been getting it right, because his stomach muscles contracted as he thrust his hips forward and he muttered darkly in French.

Reality and fantasy merged, and Jasmine didn't even have to think anymore. She just did. She lifted her face to the spray and opened her mouth, catching water until her mouth was full and leaning forward, guiding Luca into the warm bath between her lips. Displaced water gushed down her chin as she took him in.

The harsh, guttural sounds he made encouraged her to take him deeper, and then deeper still, until she couldn't breathe. Then slowly, slowly, she withdrew until his tip rested against her lips. She circled the head of him with her tongue; he tasted faintly of lavender soap and man, and it was like nothing she'd experienced before.

Better than her fantasies.

Better than—

"Jasmine..."

She'd never heard her name spoken in that tone before, with reverence, like her name could invoke magic…dark magic. Hazarding a glance up through the spray, Jasmine met Luca's lust-crazed gaze while she played his cock back and forth across her parted lips.

This was what she wanted. What she'd always dreamed about in a lover. Someone to look at her with absolute desire. She couldn't get enough. She loved the way his penis pulsed in her fist. She loved the way Luca's hands had found their way to her hair, threading though her damp tresses and holding on with a ferocity that spoke of carnal need.

She loved the savage grunts he made, seemingly against his will.

Opening her mouth wide, she took him inside again, sucking in a way she hoped matched his ferocity. This time, when she withdrew, she gently dragged her teeth along his length, not caring about whether he liked it or not, but simply doing it because *she* wanted to.

By his reaction—thrusting his hips toward her—he liked it. So she licked and sucked and trailed her nails up the inside of his thighs, beneath his balls and then down his length and Luca cried out.

"Fuck, woman." He took hold of his cock and turned himself away. Then he reached down and pulled her to her feet. "You're going to make me lose it."

"I thought that was the idea."

"Non," he said softly.

Jasmine's heart would have plummeted from insecurity if not for the obvious flame of desire in his gaze.

"I need to make you come first."

CHAPTER TEN

"YOU WANT TO…" she gasped as if the sentence was hard to finish "…make me come?"

"Yes."

She drew in a shaky breath and then exhaled again. "Do you have…condoms?" she asked, looking like some combination of innocent school girl and sultry vixen.

"Condoms?" he frowned. Then he shook his head.

She gnawed on her bottom lip. "Damn."

Pulling her body close and running his hand down the curve of her spine—better than he'd fucking imagined—he left his hand on the top of her ass and whispered, "There are plenty of ways to make you come without having to use condoms."

Because her body was so close, he felt the deep tremor that coursed through her, like his words had evoked a shock of some kind. Jesus, if simply telling her what he was going to do made her body react like this, what would this woman be like in the throes of an orgasm?

Luca couldn't wait to find out.

"But first…" He tilted her chin up and kissed her. Her mouth was warm and wet and sexy as hell. He pulled her closer and she parted her legs so that his cock fit snugly up into the warm apex of her thighs. He was so fucking tempted to simply adjust the angle and slide into her…

But not yet.

Something told him that she was not as experienced as she claimed. Could be the way her body trembled when she touched him. Or the way her eyes changed so often from a lust-filled haze to clouded with uncertainty.

With regret, he pulled back and smiled down at her. "Now…"

"Yes?"

There it was. That hopeful innocence he'd detected that told him to take it slow—now that he'd made the decision to fuck her.

"We dry off, get dressed and eat."

She blinked up at him in confusion. Oh, this was going to be both painful *and* too much fun. He ran the backs of his knuckles down her cheek and then swiped his thumb across her parted lips. She shut her eyes and automatically opened to take him in. Fuck, her mouth was to die for. So soft and sweet and innocent and sexy all at once.

"You enjoy tempting me?" he asked harshly.

Sucking deeply on his thumb—just like she'd done to his cock—she finally pulled his hand away and said, "I enjoy having parts of you inside of me. If that tempts you…" She shrugged.

And there was the other side of the coin that was Jasmine. A sexual force like a hurricane that had a calm center but could easily wreak havoc and destruction.

"Come." He took her hand and coerced her out of

the shower. There was only one towel and he dried her off first: her torso—she had pretty, dusky hued nipples, so fucking suckable. He moved down to her belly, then he dried the length of each leg before carefully rubbing the towel between. After that, he dried her hair.

She stood completely still, her lids fluttering as if she found it difficult to keep them open as she let him towel her off.

"Go get dressed," he instructed with a light slap on her bottom. "I'll meet you in the kitchen."

She blinked. There was the tiniest wrinkle between her arched brows. Then she turned and padded toward the door. She did not glance back, but she did sashay her ass in a way that was obviously meant to entice him. Her swaying backside prompted an urge to stride after her, grab her shoulder, spin her around and take her—hard—up against the door.

It would feel so fucking good.

Luca was in desperate need of release…

Non.

He would save that maneuver for later. For now, he wanted to take his time, build her arousal and get her body so fucking ready for him that she would fall apart without his even touching her.

She wore her new dress, the one she'd picked up at the shop, the one the shop girl had oohed and aahed over. It was white and sheer with spaghetti straps and a hemline that was high in the front and low in the back. It made Jasmine feel both sexy and virginal. When she swept into the kitchen, her heart beating a million miles a minute—though she did her best to maintain a cool, seductive smile—she was rewarded by a grumbling sound Luca made at the back of his throat. There was also a spark in his blue eyes and a smile that only lifted one corner of his mouth.

"You are beautiful."

It was such a simple statement. And yet the huskiness of his voice suggested he wanted to tear the fabric from her body and finish what they'd started in the bathroom.

How would he do it? How would he make her come? With his hands? His mouth?

Oh, please. Let it be with his mouth.

He'd already begun preparing a meal, and while Jasmine wanted to help—she was no slouch in the kitchen—he seemed to have things completely under control. Actually, that summed him up. Luca was a man who liked to be in control of situations. Even when he was ripping along at inhuman speeds on the motorcycle, Jasmine had known intrinsically that Luca was in *complete* control.

Supper was a thick, fluffy omelet with bits of cured meat, cheese and fresh herbs. To accompany it, Luca had opened a bottle of wine, a light white, that was absolutely delicious. They ate on the terrace as the sun began to set. Jasmine was ravenous. She hadn't eaten since breakfast.

"So," Luca said, his wine glass in hand, his eyes hooded. "Before I..." He paused. A subtle smile touched his lips as if he was thinking something irreverent—what was it?—then he changed the subject. "Tell me more about yourself."

"Before I tell you any more about myself, it's your turn to tell me a little bit about you."

Luca's posture changed from open and alluring to rigid and guarded. "There is not much to tell."

"Who are you running from?"

She didn't think he was going to answer. He stared out at the horizon and drank. Finally, he said, "I had an altercation with the police a few weeks ago."

"Are you a fugitive?"

He shrugged. "Depends on your definition."

So…she was aiding and abetting an outlaw. That thought should have terrified her. Instead, a thrill raced through her, not unlike the thrill she'd experienced on the back of his motorcycle. That, combined with the lingering arousal from the shower and the desire that Luca's mere presence elicited, meant Jasmine had never felt more alive.

"What do you do? For work?" She paused. "Or… do you work?"

He regarded her carefully as if weighing what to say. Finally he said, "I used to race motorcycles. But I don't anymore."

"So now you…?"

"I am on vacation from my job." He lifted the glass of wine. "I work for a vintner."

So that was why he knew so much about the vines in the vineyard.

"And now your turn. What do you do, when you aren't visiting Paris, losing your belongings and finding yourself concussed on a street corner?"

"You make me sound like a prostitute."

He cocked his head to one side and Jasmine couldn't decide if she should be offended or not.

"Don't look at me like that. It was not an insult."

He'd read her mind. Or perhaps he'd simply read her body language. Either way, it felt good to be read so easily by him. Like he was actually paying attention to her.

Luca refilled her glass. "Do you want to know what I think?" he asked.

"I don't know, do I?"

He set his wine glass down and reached across the table to caress the back of her hand. "I think you came to Paris looking for something."

"Why do you say that?"

"Because if given the choice between a planned vacation and a...hideout in the French countryside, most people would choose the former."

"Maybe."

"The question is, why? Why do you want to be here? With me?"

She tugged on her hand but he held it firmly. So instead of pulling away, she squeezed. "Honestly? I can't quite explain it. I just know that at this moment in time, there is nowhere I'd rather be."

Luca regarded her carefully. Though he gave very little away, the fact that his thumb caressed the back of her hand told her he was pleased by her answer. But his question did stay with her as she sipped her wine. What was it about him that compelled her to act so irrationally?

God. It was everything about him. His tone of voice—the French accent didn't hurt—his intense stares, his touch, his words, his mouth, his hands, his hard body...

Yes, it was all of that, but most of all it was the fact that he desired her.

Her.

That, in itself, was the most intoxicating thing.

124

* * *

What was it about this woman that made him so hard? She was stunning, particularly right now with her dress glowing against the darker tone of her skin and her large eyes that seemed to capture what remained of the sunset, only to reflect the light back at him. She was absolutely beautiful. But, Luca had been with beautiful women before. No. There was something else about her. Maybe it was her passion tempered with a delicious degree of innocence. Luca couldn't really pinpoint what drove him to want to give this woman what she asked for.

Non, Luca didn't want to give her what she asked for; he wanted to give her more. Much more. Starting right now. "Do you have a good imagination?"

"Excuse me?"

"Do you like to fantasize?"

Jasmine made a strange face, like she'd been caught in a lie, which was an interesting reaction.

"Everyone fantasizes, Jasmine. It is not a crime."

"I know," she said quickly, suddenly finding something very interesting about her wine glass. "Of course I fantasize about things."

"About sex?"

"Mm-hmm." It was more of a squeak than an acknowledgment.

"Tell me one."

"You want me to tell you what I fantasize about?"

"Yes. You said you aren't afraid to ask for what you want, right?"

"Yes."

"Well, our fantasies are our deepest desires. So, tell me one of yours. What is it that you want?"

Was she blushing? He reached across to touch her cheek. Jesus. She was burning up.

Why did her charming blush send blood right to his balls?

"Have you ever envisioned being tied up?" he asked when she didn't supply an answer. The question just came out, revealing more about himself than he should be sharing.

She sucked in a breath and nodded.

"Why don't you tell me about it?" he pressed.

Jasmine swirled her wine glass, thinking. Luca could hear her breaths, coming faster and faster. What was going on in her head? Was she envisioning something right now?

Softly he asked, "Have you ever imagined a man taking control of your body?"

Her gaze rose to meet his. He noted both excitement and fear in her fevered gaze.

"Are you able to trust this man in your fantasy enough to let go, so that you can experience pleasure beyond anything you've known before?"

She drew a sharp breath between her sweetly parted lips as she stared at him.

That was what this fantasy meant for Luca. It wasn't about control. It was about trust. A lover who was willing to place her pleasure in his hands was the biggest turn-on.

Maybe because trust was so very rare, in Luca's experience, as Anika and her fucking video had confirmed.

Finally, Jasmine tipped her glass to her mouth and finished her wine.

"I have imagined something along those lines," she said quietly.

"And do you trust me?"

"I do." The little wrinkle formed between her brows. "I mean, I probably shouldn't, because I barely know you." She wet her lips. "But I do."

Luca set his glass down, pushed himself to his feet and held his hand out for her to take. Jasmine's felt warm and small in his as he pulled her to her feet and walked her back inside, leading her down the hall to the master bedroom. The moment the door was shut, Jasmine turned in his arms, went up on tiptoes and kissed him.

Luca kissed her deeply before gently pushing her away. It was too easy to get carried away with this woman. If he wasn't careful, he'd have her clothes off—and his—and would find himself buried deeply inside her body before either of them knew what was happening.

Non.

He had other plans for her.

"What are you doing?" she asked as he held her at arms' length.

"I'm going to fulfill your fantasy."

"O-kay."

"And I'm going to make you come. All without touching you."

She frowned. "I don't understand."

"You will." Luca moved to an armchair that sat in the corner of the room. He dragged it closer to the bed. "You are going to do exactly as I say. Do you understand?"

She opened her mouth to reply but only ragged little breaths emerged. So she nodded her head.

"Now, take off your dress."

She stayed where she was, regarding him for a few minutes. "Why don't you take it off for me?"

"That's not how this works." He sat down and leaned back in the chair. "Take it off, Jasmine. Now."

Her arms went behind her back and she unzipped the dress. Then she nudged each strap until they hung down her arms. Finally, as if it was a sentient being, the dress slipped, slithering down her body and pooling around her feet.

Luca took a deep breath through his nose as he gazed at her in her cream-colored lace undergarments.

"Lie down on the bed and raise your hands above your head beside the pillow." He waited until she complied before continuing. "Spread your legs. Wide."

"Like this?"

"Yes." He dragged the chair closer so he could see her better. "Now, imagine your limbs are tied to the bedposts."

Jasmine rubbed her lips together. "Okay."

"You have a gag around your mouth so you may not speak. Do you understand?"

"Yes."

"You just spoke."

She nodded to show she understood.

"Good. You are waiting on the bed, blindfolded. Waiting for the sound of a man to come into the room. You are completely at his mercy. This scares you and yet excites you, as well."

She made a soft sound at the back of her throat.

"You have been fantasizing about him, though you

barely know him. You think about his hands, how it would feel if he were to touch you…"

Her fists opened and closed. Shit, she was so responsive. Of course she was.

"You have watched his lips when he speaks, wondering how they would feel, on your mouth, your breasts, your thighs…your clit."

She writhed at the mention of the word *clit*. Luca smiled. "But it is his cock that keeps you up at night. You can't stop thinking about it. Longing to know how it would feel in your hand. The skin. The tip. The weight of his balls. You hunger to taste it, to suck it gently into your mouth, to explore it with your tongue. But most of all, your pussy aches with the need to feel it rammed up inside of you. Slowly at first, wonderfully, painfully slow, until you cry out for more and only then, when you are on the verge of tears, does he slam it home…"

Her hands clenched the comforter and her legs strained against invisible bonds. She shifted her ass. Why? To create friction to ease some secret itch?

Luca's body responded to hers. His dick throbbed behind the denim of his jeans. He popped the button and let the zipper slide open. "The door opens and someone comes in. It's the man. You can tell by his footsteps. He is there in the room with you."

Jasmine moaned.

Fuck.

Luca shoved his hand down the front of his jeans, needing to pull himself free. He was so fucking hard it hurt.

"Would you like me to tell you what he's going to do to you?"

She didn't say yes. That would be breaking the rules of the fantasy. But her answer—nodding her head while making needy sounds at the back of her throat—was clearly consent.

Jasmine's body was on fire. No one had ever spoken to her like this before. Not even close.

"He gazes down at you, naked and tied to his bed. His to do with as he pleases."

She sucked in a breath. Why did that statement excite her? It shouldn't…but it did. It did so much.

"He has watched you, touched you, even kissed you, and now he is going to have you. Just the way he wants you."

Oh, God. Maybe this was too much…

"He starts with the toes on your left foot. Painted so prettily, like little candies."

He'd noticed her toe nail polish?

"Sitting on the foot of the bed, he caresses your toes before leaning down to suck on each one, drawing them into his warm mouth. Your body responds violently and with pleasure."

Jasmine's hips flew off the bed in response to the imagery. Her toes sucked? She'd never imagined such a thing. But now? She could practically feel it. Warm and wet, his mouth lapping at her. Sucking on her.

"He touches your feet, made more sensitive by the bonds, the bottoms, the tops, your ankles, before sliding his hands up your calves and thighs. You moan as he caresses higher and higher. Showing him where you want him to touch by the way you lift your hips off the bed."

It was like he was there. She could feel him kneeling between her legs, and her clit throbbed with the idea that she was spread before him.

"Your bare pussy is exquisite and he lightly strokes over your mound, dragging the backs of his knuckles over your clit. Circling the inside of your thighs and lightly pressing just the tips of his fingers into your wet heat."

Oh, God.

"So soft. So warm. He leans over and breathes hot air against you as you strain your hips toward his mouth. Wanting touch. Wanting that mouth to suck on you. Lick you. Penetrate you."

Holy…fuck. She lifted her hips toward this imaginary lover. Needing…

"But you are his captive. His prisoner to torture and tease. He nudges your swollen clit with the tip of his tongue before moving on, enjoying the sound of your muffled cries of frustration."

Jasmine grunted.

"He drags his fingers up from your hips, past your belly, clutching your sides so he can lean down and play inside the sweet indent of your navel. Your hips strain beneath him, your pussy jealous of the way he licks your belly and of the attention he gives to your breasts, pinching your pretty nipples, preparing them for his mouth."

Oh, God, oh, God…

"Slowly he continues in an upward direction, kissing and licking your sides, your rib cage beneath your breasts, circling round and round until he finds a nipple made taut by his fingers."

Her breasts ached as if they had been fondled, but not hard enough…

"No touching. Put your hands back up over your head, Jasmine, or I won't finish."

Dammit. She hadn't even noticed she'd done that, but her breasts were so sensitive, so needy.

"He sucks on one nipple and then the other. He sucks hard and you cry out. While he does that, he places a knee between your parted thighs and grinds back and forth across your swollen cunt."

That word. No one had ever used that word with her before. She hadn't thought she liked it, but…now? Now her pussy wept at the carnal image the word painted.

"You're so fucking wet, you're staining the knee of his jeans with your arousal."

Jasmine gasped; her pussy throbbed.

"The man slides to the side so that he is propped beside you, gazing down at your perfect body, caressing you with his gaze before giving in to the need to touch, following the cords down your neck to your collarbones and your breasts, barely skimming his fingers over your skin, leaving gooseflesh in his wake.

"He plays with you, draws circles and patterns across your breasts and abdomen before finally hovering just above your mound. You lift your head, as if to see. Needing to watch when he finally buries his fingers inside of you. But the blindfold prohibits it and you moan with frustration."

With her eyes closed, Jasmine enacted his words, lifting her head off the bed as if unable to see her lover lying between her legs.

"He needs to taste you. He's longed to suck the sweet honey from your pretty pussy lips, so swollen and rosy with desire."

A soft whine formed at the back of her throat as a

tingling sensation that simultaneously started at the tips of her fingers and toes rushed through her limbs to coalesce low in her belly.

"He spreads you even wider, holding you open with his thumbs and then leans in for a taste. Lapping along your slit, sucking on you and fucking you with his tongue…"

Oh, shit…oh, shit…

The tingling, throbbing mass swirling in her abdomen exploded, tugging on all her parts until Jasmine swore she'd disintegrate. Crying out, she clutched at her throbbing crotch with both hands in an unsuccessful attempt to quell the orgasm raging through her.

"That's it, Jasmine. Come for me."

Her eyes popped open.

She was lying on the bed, legs splayed, still wearing her bra and panties. Luca stood over her, his cock in his hand, stroking.

"Did you like it?" he asked, his voice gruff.

"Yes," she managed, keeping one hand clamped between her legs and reaching for him with her other hand.

He stepped closer and let her cover his hand with hers.

"I'm going to come on your belly. Is that okay?"

"Oh, fuck, yes."

He grunted. Placed a knee on the edge of the bed and pumped his cock like a piston. Jasmine could barely keep up with the pace. But she knew he was close by the sounds he was making and by the pained expression that flicked over his features.

"Jesus," he muttered darkly. Then he leaned over her, gripped his cock and spewed come into a hot pool across her stomach and rib cage. He remained poised above her for a few breaths before zipping himself up and telling her to stay where she was.

He returned moments later with a warm, damp cloth to wipe her clean. When he was done, he left her once again.

"Wait," Jasmine called before he shut the door behind him. "Where are you going?"

"To sleep in the other room."

"Why?"

He stood in the open doorway, just a dark shadow. Finally he said, "I can't sleep beside you without fucking you."

He didn't wait for her answer. He simply closed the door and left her to her own thoughts.

Aftershocks continued to quiver through her already trembling body. She'd just had an orgasm. An amazing, body-shattering, mind-blowing orgasm. But more than that, she'd had it without any physical stimulation whatsoever, not from him and not from herself.

He'd made her come with words.

Maybe people did this all the time. With phone sex and stuff. But Jasmine had never had phone sex. In fact, she'd never had an orgasm with a man present.

Period.

God, Jazz...if you came that hard just by him talking to you...imagine what it would be like to really be with him. To do all the crazy things you've fantasized about.

"I don't think my imagination is even capable," she whispered to herself in the dark. Shedding her bra and panties, Jasmine crawled naked between the sheets. She lay on her back staring at the dark ceiling. She should have felt elated at the notion of being with Luca, but she'd realized something very important. Luca was clearly an expert in bed.

What would he do when he found out she wasn't?

CHAPTER ELEVEN

IT WAS WEDNESDAY MORNING. Luca rose early and the first thing he did was drive to the nearby village of La Charité-sur-Loire to pick up a few things that Monsieur Gauthier had missed. Namely, toiletries and condoms.

Merde.

It had taken him a while to fall asleep last night, knowing Jasmine lay sleeping just down the hall. Her responsive body primed and ready for him.

She was probably still soaking wet.

Now, ten hours later, the thought of her wet pussy made Luca's dick instantly hard. Yet he still wanted to take things slow. It was so rare to find a woman his age who was both ready and willing to engage in exploratory sex but was still relatively innocent—for whatever reason.

It was a mystery. Jasmine was a gorgeous, sophisticated woman who obviously enjoyed sex. So why was she so fucking innocent?

Do you really care?

He shouldn't care, but strangely, Luca did.

He parked his bike at the pharmacy, debating about whether to leave his helmet on or not. He didn't want to risk anyone recognizing him. It had been many years since he'd been here, and with his beard and grown-out hair, he didn't look like the Luca Legrand in all the promotional pictures and from the tabloids. Still, he couldn't take the chance. He simply raised his visor, went inside and picked up the items he needed.

There was an elderly man behind the counter, and when he glanced at Luca there was no sign of recognition. Thank God.

A few more stops and Luca was on his way back to the villa. When he got back, he smelled freshly brewed coffee and something being fried in butter.

"Morning," Jasmine said over her shoulder. "Where have you been?"

In different circumstances, he might have felt annoyed by the question. Who was she to question his whereabouts? But he didn't feel annoyed. He only felt one thing.

Aroused.

He came right up behind her, wrapped his arm around her waist—she was wearing a skirt and tank top—lifted her mane of hair and kissed her neck. "I was buying some necessities." He plopped the paper sack on the counter in front of her.

Jasmine reached inside, squealing with thanks over the shampoo, conditioner, hairbrush and soap.

"Oh…" she said, dragging out the vowel. "What's this?" She held up a box of condoms. "Twenty-four?"

Luca didn't make any excuses; he just smiled, pulled her close and slid his hand up the inside of her thigh. That was all it took for her to melt against him, her body molded to his, her hands on his forearms. "Luca?"

"Mmm." He nuzzled his face into the curve of her neck and shoulder.

"I need to tell you something."

Her voice was flat and serious. He released her and backed up a step to regard her but she avoided eye contact.

"What is it?"

"Can we talk while we eat?"

"Of course."

She poured him the coffee—nice and strong, which was a pleasant surprise—then slid eggs onto a plate with a slab of toasted bread and sliced tomatoes.

Sitting across from him at the kitchen table, she fiddled with her utensils. Shit. She was about to confess something.

What?

"I'm not who you think I am."

Okay, that wasn't what he'd expected her to say. He took a bite of egg, pretending not to be surprised, and then washed it down with a gulp of coffee. "You mean, you're not American?"

She chuckled softly. "That's not what I mean." She took a small bite of bread that took an overly long time to chew. "I mean, I'm not as experienced as you."

Luca hid his smile. Did she think he didn't already know that? "Really?" He drank more coffee, watching her. She kept her gaze averted and suddenly Luca had a flash of what she was going to confess.

"Jesus," he said, putting his coffee cup down. "You're a virgin."

She shook her head. "No. I'm not." But the little lines between her arched brows told a different story.

Fuck. How did he feel about that? It was a shock, that was for sure. Yet...his cock twitched at the notion, as if excited by the prospect. Not good. As much as some primal part of him celebrated the idea of being the first man to claim this incredible woman, his logical side kicked in. This was supposed to be a meaningless tryst—just a bit of fucking—only for a couple of days. It wasn't supposed to be an initiation.

That was too…meaningful.

She slid her hand across the table and covered his. Her fingers trembled and now he understood those tremors. "Jasmine, I don't think it's a good idea if we continue—"

"Wait. Don't say it." She finally met his gaze, her large brown eyes pleading with him. "I'm not a virgin, but…" She pulled her hand away and made a harsh sound at the back of her throat. "God, it's so…"

"What?"

"The last man I was with, actually, he was the only man I've ever been with. And…"

"And?"

"Well, he…" She paused, and her face contorted in pain.

Oh, fuck. Some shithead had hurt her? This was worse and he should be packing her up and driving her to the train station. Right now. But, instead, he took hold of her chin and forced her to look at him. For some odd reason, his gut clenched and his other hand grasped his knife as if he meant to use it as a weapon. "Tell me," he growled.

"He used me." She shrugged and tried to turn away.

Luca didn't let her. "What does that mean?"

"God, Luca. Do I have to say it?"

"Yes." He ground his teeth.

Jasmine stood up and moved to the sink, turning her back to him. He pushed his chair away and fol-

lowed her, going to stand right behind her, though he
didn't touch her.

"He pretended to be something he wasn't. He used
me to keep up his facade."

"And what facade was that?"

She leaned against the counter. "That he was
straight."

It took a moment for her words to sink in. Then,
with hands placed gently on her shoulders, Luca turned
Jasmine to face him. "Are you telling me that the only
man you've ever been with was gay?"

She bit her lip and nodded her head.

"And this man…" Luca suddenly thought of the ring
that he'd tucked in his wallet. "Was he your fiancé?"

She nodded, her lip quivering. "I walked in on him.
With his best man."

Jesus.

Luca gazed down into her tortured eyes. A voice in
his head—that sounded suspiciously like François—
was telling him this woman was damaged and that he
should stay away from her. That continuing any kind
of sexual tryst was taking advantage of her vulner-
ability. But Luca didn't want to stay away. Fuck, no.
He wanted to enfold her in his arms and hold her. He
wanted to kiss away the tears that glistened at the corners of her eyes and to tell her that this other man was
a *salaud*, a bastard, for trying to use her. More impor-
tantly, he wanted to show her how beautiful she was,
how desirable she was, and to teach her the absolute
joys of making love to someone who couldn't contain
his lust for her.

So he settled on something somewhere in between
those two extremes. He held both sides of her face and

leaned down to kiss her softly. Then he backed away and said, "I think it's time we explore this passion between us, don't you?"

Her lips trembled when she smiled, and Luca experienced a bizarre combination of tenderness, desire and dread.

Jasmine wanted to be thoroughly and completely fucked by this man, but she also wanted him to know what to expect—or not to expect—from her. She had been terrified to tell Luca the truth. Had stayed up half the night trying to figure out what to say or whether she should just go on pretending to be someone she wasn't. But when she saw that box of condoms, she'd known she had to come clean.

Now she was so glad she had. He kissed her. Sweetly. Then he grabbed the box of condoms and led her back to the bedroom.

Her legs felt wobbly as she stood there, watching him hang his leather jacket on the back of a chair. Her knees nearly gave out when he stalked back to her, his hair mussed, his gaze intent, his jaw firm. He yanked her close and threaded his fingers through her hair, holding her head steady for what he was about to do, which was to devour her mouth until she couldn't breathe. His lips were everywhere. On her lips, on her cheek, in her ear, on her neck, back on her mouth, inside her mouth. Not just kissing but biting and licking, sucking and owning.

She pulled away, not because she wanted to stop but because she needed a moment to catch her breath. After a lungful of air he moved them forward, easing her onto her back, dragging her up onto the comforter beneath him.

"You have driven me crazy from the very first, do you know that?" His words were dark and dangerous as he kneeled above her, gazing at her like he didn't want to just devour her lips but her entire body.

Yes. Yes, please.

"Knowing you were here in this bedroom last night was torture." He tugged the front of her top up, taking her bra with it, exposing her bare breasts and licking his lips like she was dinner. "Watching you come was my undoing." His hands moved to her legs, pushing the skirt up and up until it was gathered at her waist, revealing her white panties.

"Jesus. Are all of your undergarments fucking virginal?" He groaned.

"I like white. And I'm not a virgin."

He slid his hands up between her legs, parted them and then moved in between. He kneaded her upper thighs, sliding higher until his thumbs reached beneath the lace of her panties. "Do you know that first night I lay on my couch thinking about this? Thinking about the texture of your skin, the taste of your pussy. How soft and wet you'd be."

Did he mean it? Jasmine didn't know, but the way he looked at her was intoxicating and made her girl parts tremble with the need to climax.

He caressed over the white lace, slipping fingers under and grunting with pleasure as he explored between her folds.

"I can't decide if I want to fuck you with these panties on or not."

A fiery bolt of electricity slammed through her at

his suggestion. The idea that he'd shove part of the lace
aside and enter her that way was so erotic. God, she
loved the way he talked dirty to her.

Her body reacted to his words and his touch, her
hips meeting his hands, gyrating against his fingers.
Wanting what he was doing but wanting more, too.

"Take them off. Please."

He granted her wish, but when he revealed the bare
skin beneath, it was as if it pained him because something sharp flashed across his features. After tossing
the panties to the side, he spread her wide and slid two
fingers into her body until his knuckles bumped against
her clit. Lowering himself to her side, he observed her
expression as he twisted and pulsed inside of her.

"Do you like being finger fucked?"

"Yes," she said, her voice sounding on the verge of
a sob. "I love it."

There was that expression again. Like this was hurt-
ing him.

With her free hand, she smoothed the wrinkle from
between his brow and whispered, "Harder. Do it harder.
Please."

He made a low rumbling in his chest but he gave
her want she wanted, withdrawing his hand and then
slamming his fingers back inside, watching her carefully the whole time.

"Oh, yes!" Her hips flew off the bed. The pressure
his fingers created, the friction, the growl he made
as he did these things to her. He was enjoying this as
much as she was.

"Mon Dieu."

To Jasmine's dismay, he pulled his hand away,

though what he did next made it okay. Bringing his fingers to his nose, he inhaled deeply before licking them.

But when he pushed one of her legs wider so he could crawl back in between her thighs, she wriggled with the knowledge of what was about to happen. Her favorite thing to fantasize about. The very thing she'd never done before.

Could she do it? Could she let him…?

Too late.

He spread her wide and then buried his head between her thighs, feasting on her. That was the only way to describe it. She grasped his thick hair with both hands. Seeing him there, the top of his head and dark hair positioned between her legs, the feel of his tongue, teasing her clit before sucking on her, his thumbs sharing entry inside of her, was all more than she could take.

"Luca…" she moaned, clutching at his hair. Desperate. "Please." Please what? She had no fucking clue. She just knew she needed something.

He didn't let go but rather increased the pressure on her, moving his head back and forth rapidly, penetrating her with his tongue and fingers together. Then… oh, yes…he squeezed his pinky finger into the tight opening of her ass, something no one had ever done, something she hadn't been sure she'd ever like.

She didn't like it; she *loved* it.

Her pussy erupted inside his mouth, her body bucking out of control with the severity of her orgasm as she kicked and tugged frantically at his hair.

"Luca…yes, yes, oh, God, yes!"

Jasmine thought she might start crying, not out of sadness but out of the weight of release. It was Luca who slowed things down, who cupped her pussy, holding on to the aftershocks of her orgasm as if he was going to keep them for later. He crawled up beside her, stroking her face, calming her until she opened her eyes and saw him there, watching her.

Softly he kissed her, his mouth so warm and tasting of sweet sex.

"You are a beautiful woman," he said softly. "But when you come? You are a fucking goddess."

How had this amazing woman never experienced oral sex before? He'd known she was not as experienced as she claimed, yet she'd given him an un-fucking-believable blow job yesterday in the shower.

"Thank you," she whispered.

"For kissing you?"

She nodded, smiling shyly.

"Did you like it?"

"Yes." Her smile faltered as she tugged her wrinkled shirt back over her breasts.

"What are you doing?"

"Getting dressed."

"Why?"

"Because—"

Oh, no, she wasn't. "Come here." He rolled off the bed and extended his hand, offering to help her up. She took it and stood, uncertain, her skirt hanging askew around her hips.

"We are not done here, Jasmine."

"We're not?"

"That was only the entrée." He licked his lips, her flavor still lingering there. Fucking delicious.

"But, isn't the entrée the main course?"

"No." He lifted her shirt up and off, and tugged the skirt down her hips so that it fell about her bare feet. "In France, the entrée is only the first course."

"Oh."

Lord, he could gaze at her naked body forever. Her skin had a beautiful rosy flush to it that was in delicious contrast to her dark hair.

"So, now what?"

"Now you are going to do exactly as I say."

Her gaze flew up to his, her swollen lips parted, his words and meaning making her gasp. Not in fear, but in excitement and willingness.

"Undress me."

Her brows rose and then she nodded, her fingers moving quickly to the buttons on his linen shirt.

"Not so fast. Enjoy every moment."

With her fingers on the third button, she gazed at it before slowly slipping the button through the hole. She moved on to the next and he felt the pressure of her fingernails on his skin.

Divine.

She continued, as if the act of buttons coming free of their buttonholes was fascinating, until his shirt was undone and she parted it like a curtain at the start of a play. The soft grunt she made after running her hands over his bare chest elicited a growl from him. Her touch was so wonderfully erotic. Tentative and sensual all at once.

"My God," she murmured as she leaned close and rubbed her cheek against him. "You have the nicest chest."

The statement made his already hard cock twitch.

"And you smell delicious." She ran her tongue in

between his pecs and then circled one of his nipples before lightly clamping her teeth on the other. "Taste even better."

For an inexperienced woman, there were times when she sure as hell seemed to know what she was doing. Luca fought the urge to twist her lush hair around his fists and to position her where he wanted her. But that was *not* what he wanted, not for Jasmine, anyway. He wanted to savor every fucking moment, which meant he had to control his more basic urges—no easy feat when the mere sight of her made him desperate to bury his cock in her warm body. But taking his time and building anticipation always made it better, and that was what he wanted for her.

Maybe there would come a time when she would welcome some of the other forms of lovemaking he enjoyed, where he could express his more dominant side. The idea drove him to distraction, but for this first time…

Wait.

How many times would they be doing this?

Well, you did buy twenty-four condoms…

He had, but he also had other things to worry about and this—whatever this was—couldn't last more than a couple of days. Jasmine needed to get back to her own life.

Jasmine's hands brought him back to the here and now as she slipped them beneath the shoulders of his shirt, pushing it off and tugging on the sleeves so the garment fell to the floor.

Her hands fluttered down his arms and back up again. Her soft pants were audible in the quiet room and Luca held himself perfectly still as she explored the terrain of his body.

"Do you like touching me?"

"Yes."

"Had you thought about it, while you were in my bed at the apartment?"

Her hands stilled and she slowly raised her gaze. "Maybe."

"Did you wonder if I had plans to…touch you?"

"Yes."

"Did that excite you?"

"Yes." She slid her hands up his chest to his shoulders, following the line of his collarbone. Up his neck her fingers went, to his jaw. "But I was worried, too…"

"Worried about what?"

"That you didn't want me."

He took her hand, kissed her fingers and directed them down his chest to the fly of his jeans. "I want you."

"Oh, my God…" she whispered reverently as she squeezed his erection.

"Undo my belt."

Eagerly, her hands whipped the leather through the loop but he covered her hands again. "Slowly."

She tightened the leather in order to release the prong before sliding the belt off him completely. It made a wonderful hissing sound sliding through the loops and brought to mind other ways he wouldn't mind using the belt.

Not yet.

Once the belt was on the floor, her hands rested on the waistband of his jeans. Could she feel his cock twitching beneath the fabric? Luca wanted her to both hurry the fuck up *and* keep up the leisurely pace of this slow-dance prelude to lovemaking.

Carefully, she popped the top button before slowly unzipping his fly and parting the fabric to push it down his hips.

"Shorts, too."

His cock needed to be free. That was all there was to it.

Fitting her hands beneath the material, she pushed shorts and jeans down his hips, kneeling in front of him—oh, God—while she tugged his clothes all the way down his legs.

Did she have any idea how erotic that was, her kneeling before him, her gorgeous mouth in line with his erection? Looking up at him with such willingness— just like she had in the shower—like she'd do whatever the fuck he asked? His erection bobbed at the notion, straining toward her as she slipped her hands back up his calves, the backs of his knees, pausing on the front of his thighs, not touching him. Yet.

"You're so…"

"So what?"

"Hard."

Oh, fuck. She wrapped that small hand of hers around his cock and squeezed. Luca hadn't had such a sustained erection for so many days and just the simple act of her touch was more than he could take.

"Get a condom from the box and put it on me."

She didn't move, like she hadn't heard him, and licked her lips as if she wanted a taste. No. He would explode in her mouth if she did that. He was way too fucking close.

"Do it now, Jasmine," he commanded through gritted teeth.

His tone broke through to her and she obeyed, getting up and returning quickly with a condom between her fingers.

The fact she was so adept at rolling it over his length meant she'd done this before. She'd said as much, so why did that thought disturb him?

"Lie down on the bed. Spread your legs."

He couldn't help it; his dominant side was taking over, but Jasmine didn't seem to mind. No, in fact, she seemed to be enjoying this. Her pretty little nipples were tight with arousal and the smell of her drifted through his senses, her own personal scent made stronger by the warmth of her flushed skin.

"Show me your pussy."

God, she had the most beautiful cunt he'd ever seen. Rosy and swollen, and when she pulled her pussy lips open, she revealed the most delicious pink center, covered in a lovely sheen of arousal.

He needed her.

He needed her right fucking now.

CHAPTER TWELVE

OH, GOD. JASMINE had never needed something so badly in her life. Luca towered over her, magnificently male, deliciously nude, his face inscrutable, his fists opening and closing at his sides. What her eyes were drawn to most, however, was that *very* male part of him that rose erect and proud from his groin.

"Please," she said in between pants, as she fondled herself.

He crawled onto the bed, moving on top of her, making her feel so small and feminine beneath his bulk. With one hand wrapped around the back of her neck, he raised her face to kiss her. Deeply. His mouth was warm and commanding as he moved leisurely over hers. But when she slipped her tongue between his lips, he groaned and his hips ground in between hers, forcing her thighs wide, adjusting so the tip of him was situated right at her entrance.

"Please, Luca."

The kiss deepened. His hips shifted and then…oh!

He was inside of her—finally!—filling her wholly and completely. Her body reacted like a bow pulled taut, arching against him while the entire length of his penis created beautiful friction moving all the way up inside.

"Ahh." He sighed into her hair, holding himself flush for a second before slowly withdrawing again. "So good."

He nuzzled her neck and her temple while he supported himself on one arm and Jasmine clutched that arm, marveling at the sheer power of this man.

So sexy.

What was even sexier was when he backed up onto his knees so she could see him, the sheen of sweat on his chest, the play of muscles across his taut abdomen that danced while he thrust between her parted thighs.

"You are incredibly beautiful," he murmured. His gaze settled at the point where their bodies joined and the thrusts increased in tempo while he watched himself drive in and out of her. Jasmine couldn't decide if it was sexier watching him disappear inside or watching the passion on his face.

Suddenly his expression changed from passion to purpose and his tempo increased. Everything he did was unexpected, three quick thrusts followed by one hard one followed by a slow withdrawal.

So good. So, so good.

He shifted, releasing her ass to reach for her legs, placing them flat against his chest, her ass flush with his hips. Gazing down at her, he kissed one instep and then the other, reminding Jasmine of how he'd talked about sucking on her toes. Was he going to do that now? Her pussy pulsed in anticipation.

He didn't. Oh, no.

Instead, he raised her ass, leaned forward and...

"Oh!" she cried with wonder.

The position created friction in new and sensitive places and the pressure inside of her swelled as he leaned into her upright legs, bending her in half while his cock drove into her again and again.

"Luca," she moaned because he hit a part of her that sent a frisson of pleasure to the tips of her toes and the crown of her head. Release gushed between her thighs and she cried out again. This was not an orgasm; this was something else, something that had never happened to her before.

"Jesus..." he muttered, holding her legs tight and moving in short, sharp bursts before finally parting her thighs and lowering himself on top of her, moving at a frenetic pace as he watched her face.

"Come for me, Jasmine. I want to see you come."

"I already did. I don't know if I can again."

He guided her hand down between them.

"See how wet you are? How much your pussy likes this?"

Oh, God.

"Play with your clit while I fuck you. Make yourself come for me. I want to feel it while I'm inside of you."

She pinched herself, though she didn't need to. His words alone were enough to push her over the edge, tension from her core, her ass, her thighs and that new, oh-so-sweet spot inside of her, all strained together at once before releasing simultaneously in a cataclysmic wave of rapture.

"Yes, oh, fuck, yes." He urged her on as he increased the pace, driving into her harder and faster until Jasmine couldn't breathe. Until she couldn't take it anymore because it all felt so good. Too good.

And just when she thought he couldn't go harder,

he did, and instead of abating, her orgasm expanded, sending shockwaves up into her chest and down her thighs to the backs of her knees.

"Luca!"

He growled in response, gripping her hips and driving into her one last time before squeezing his eyes shut and shouting something in French.

The woman was insatiable. Was there any wonder? She was a passionate, sensual being who had never been able to express that part of her. So Luca had no problem with the fact that they spent the next five days in bed. He warned her she might feel sore, but she never complained.

Probably because she was always so fucking wet.

They'd laundered their clothes and hung them on the line to dry—they should really pick up some more—but so far they'd had very little need for clothing. Their last few days had consisted of waking up, fucking, eating, showering, fucking, napping, eating…fucking.

He still had another week before he could return to his normal life. The Legrand champagne had increased in value thanks to the magic of Myra Monte, and his absence hadn't hurt. Checking the prices was the only thing he'd used his cell phone for, which he only did every other day now. If he had to bide his time out of the limelight, then spending it in bed with Jasmine wasn't the worst way to do it.

The only problem was, he needed Jasmine to go back to her own life at some point. So why did the thought of her leaving create a strange ache in the pit of his stomach?

Maybe because she had helped him forget about

the pain he had always associated with this villa and the loss of his mother. Or maybe it was because, for the first time since his mother had died, Luca felt as if someone saw him for who he truly was. Not Luca Legrand the hotshot Grand Prix motorcycle racer. Not Luca Legrand the heir to a fortune.

Just Luca.

It was late afternoon, and they were lying in bed after another hot and heavy session. Her body was warm and pliant in his arms, and while she was drowsy, he could tell by her breathing that she was still awake.

There was nowhere else Luca wanted to be at that moment. Not even on the racetrack. Holy shit. That was saying something.

Jasmine shifted in his arms and reached for the box that stood open on the nightstand. She pulled out the line of condoms, counted them and then stuffed them back inside. "We have four left. You know what that means?"

"We've used twenty?"

"Your math skills are astounding." She laughed. "Do you think we should get some more?"

"At the rate you're going, we'll need more by the end of the day."

She slapped him playfully on the chest before lying back down. "I never imagined it'd be this way," Jasmine said quietly, lost in thought as she lazily drew lines up and down the length of his torso.

When he didn't respond, she continued, "I mean, I'd imagined it…lots of times. All the time, actually. But I kind of thought it wasn't real. That maybe I was deviant because I thought about sex all the time, you know?" She propped her chin on her hand so she could gauge Luca's expression. "I didn't think people really did it this much. Is it normal?"

He stroked the hair at the side of her head. "Yes, it's normal. And you are not deviant." His smile grew. "Well...maybe a little, but the good kind of deviant."

She returned his smile and laid her head back down, pressing her ear to his chest. Was she listening to his heartbeat? He pulled her closer, liking the idea.

"Is it like this with other men?"

A grumble erupted deep inside of his chest. "Other men?"

"Are all men like you?" She shifted onto his shoulder so she could see his face. "Do they like doing it as much as you?"

The deep, rumbly sound inside of him intensified.

"Why are you growling?" she asked, propping herself up again.

"I'm not growling."

She patted his chest. "Yes, you are."

He lifted his head and gazed at her. His smile had disappeared and he felt his nostrils flare.

"Are you angry?"

"I'm not angry. I just don't know how to answer your question. I don't think about the sex lives of other men."

"Well, you've been with other women, obviously." She flopped back down. "A lot, I'm sure."

Jesus. What was wrong with him? Why did her semijealous tone gladden him, and why the hell did the thought of her going out and having amazing sex with someone else drive him to want to punch something?

In the throat.

"Can I tell you something?"

"Yes." He hoped she was changing the subject because this topic was aggravating him.

"There's something I remember, before the whole robbery thing in that shop in Paris, it might be the last thing I remember…"

Luca's stomach tightened and his arm twitched beneath her.

She propped herself up on his chest. "I remember this lamp. It was an antique silver lamp that reminded me so much of these stories my aunt used to tell to me and my cousins. *Arabian Nights*." Her eyes lit with remembrance.

"Oh?" Luca relaxed his arms and exhaled a breath he'd been holding.

"I rubbed it." She smiled with a faraway look. "Almost like I expected a genie to appear and grant me three wishes." She met his gaze and stroked his jaw where his beard had gotten thicker. "I think it must have worked."

Luca laughed. "You think I'm a magical genie?"

"I think what you do to me is magical and I'm pretty sure I've been granted more than my share of wishes."

He snuggled her closer. "You sure you don't have any unanswered wishes or…desires?" They'd just made love and yet Luca's cock stirred at the thought of trying something new.

"Well…" Her expression changed from thoughtful to playful. "Remember when you asked me about my fantasies?"

"I might remember a conversation about fantasies." Luca was purposefully vague.

She laid her head back down on his chest and drew circles on his abdomen. "I have this one fantasy…"

Seriously. He should be exhausted. Spent. There should not be one ounce of arousal left in him. But for Jasmine? There was. "I want to hear this fantasy."

"I loved fairy tales as a kid. They've sort of informed my adult fantasies."

"Is that so?"

"Yes. And there's one where I'm dressed in a red cloak…"

"Like Little Red Riding Hood?"

"Maybe." She lifted her head. The uncertainty that he hadn't seen in a couple of days had returned. "Is that silly?"

"No. Tell me more."

Her gaze slid to the side, recalling. "I'm walking through the forest and… I'm being followed."

"By a wolf?"

She shook her head. "No. By a man." She stroked his face. "I've always been more fixated on the huntsman than the wolf. Of course, he's a shirtless man with a beard."

"I am shirtless. I also have a beard. That is an interesting coincidence."

"Yes." She bit her lower lip.

"And then what happens?"

"He chases me."

"Does he catch you?"

She nodded.

"And once he catches you?"

"He eats me. There's a bit of wolf in him, after all."

Luca groaned. His cock was rock hard.

"But first, he ties me up…"

How was it possible the woman had just described one of his own favorite fantasies? Easing her body off his, Luca rolled from the bed and went in search of something to wear. He bent down to grab a damp towel left discarded after their morning shower and fixed it around his hips.

"Where are you going?" she called.

"To get our clothes from the line. And then you're going to town to find yourself a red cloak."

She hadn't found a red cloak when she took the bicycle to the village to shop, so she'd settled on a red dress, instead. In addition to that, she'd picked up some new underwear. Not that she was wearing any right now.

"Put on the dress," Luca had commanded after she'd arrived back at the villa. He'd insisted on staying behind for who knew what reason.

Whatever the reason, it had evoked goose bumps along her arms despite the warm weather.

Jasmine had gulped. God, she loved it when he was authoritative. Maybe because she knew what it meant. He was going to take control of her body and give her the most mind-blowing gift of pleasure imaginable.

"Oh, and Jasmine," he'd said over his shoulder. "Don't bother with panties."

Now Jasmine was out in the garden behind the house picking fruit. Clouds were gathering overhead and a breeze lifted the skirt of her dress and caressed her nether regions in a delightful way, reminding her of her pantylessness. She didn't feel exposed, however—she felt positively content.

No. Not content.

Alive.

Electric.

Sensual.

Luca had said she would know when he was about to pursue her, but he didn't tell her how she would know.

"Go out into the garden and wait for my signal."

"What signal?" she'd asked.

"You'll know when you hear it."

"And then what?"

He'd smiled wickedly. "And then you run…"

She took a bite out of a pear she'd just picked. It wasn't ripe yet and was bitter on her tongue. That was when she heard the engine of Luca's motorcycle roar to life.

Oh, shit!

He wasn't supposed to pursue her by motorcycle. That was cheating!

Jasmine dropped the pear and dove behind a tree. Already her heart was beating like crazy and her palms were sweating. She peeked around the trunk of the tree, and when she didn't see any sign of man or motorcycle, she made a run for the boathouse, about seventy yards from where she had been crouching. When she got to the boathouse she tried the door. It was locked.

Damn.

She shouldn't be breathing so hard after running such a short distance but she could barely catch her breath. Talk about fantasy and reality merging. There was no reason to be frightened. It was only Luca out there, and they were merely playing a game—her game—this wasn't real.

But it felt real.

Maybe because she didn't know what he would do to her once he caught her. The one thing Jasmine had no doubt about was the fact that Luca *would* catch her. Particularly given he was on the motorcycle. Pressing

her body against the wall, she maneuvered around to
the back of the structure. Only once she was on the far
side did she hazard a quick glance around the corner of
the wall to see if there was any sign of Luca.

Nothing.

However, the sound of the bike was louder.

Where the hell was he?

She needed a plan.

The dovecote was about fifty yards away to the east.
In the opposite direction was a meadow of wild flowers
and beyond that was the overgrown vineyard. That's
where he would expect her to go.

So, where should she go? Should she be predictable
or should she play for real, attempting to evade him?

She leaned against the wooden wall and listened.
The sound of the bike changed. He was on the move.
She pressed a hand against her churning stomach and
shut her eyes.

"Okay, Jazz. This is your fantasy. If you're going to
play, you're playing for real, got it?"

She took a deep breath and peeped around the corner again. The sound of the engine was definitely moving in the direction of the vineyard. Dovecote it was,
then. She slid along the wall toward the eastern corner
and then, when she was positive the coast was clear,
she dashed out into the open, heading for the cylindri-
cal structure. It was shaded by large walnut trees, and
soon Jasmine felt protected by the cover of foliage.
There was no door on the crumbling building, just a
rectangular opening, and she ducked inside.

Light filtered in through openings in the conical
roof and Jasmine stared up in wonder. There must have
been at least two or three hundred nesting sites hon-

eycombed into the walls, all empty now. She'd never seen anything like it.

What would it have looked like filled with birds?

Suddenly the sound of the bike grew closer and Jasmine realized she'd chosen a hiding place with only one entrance. Her heart pounded against her rib cage as if trapped and desperate to get out.

The bike drew closer, driving slowly. He was in the garden now.

Shit!

It was difficult to breathe.

Jasmine searched the interior of the structure. There was a small ledge halfway up the wall. Maybe if she climbed the nests she could hide on the ledge. She tested a stone pocket that had served as a nesting site. It seemed solid enough.

The sound of the bike came closer and Jasmine held her breath.

Shit. He was right outside!

Without another thought, she began to climb. It was easier than it looked, the little ledges for the nests made the perfect hand- and footholds. It would have been even easier if her palms weren't so damp from sweat. She could see the ledge up above almost within reach. A couple more feet.

Then Jasmine realized something. At first she hadn't noticed because of the blood pounding between her ears, but now, suddenly, she did.

Silence.

Luca had turned off his bike.

She glanced down to find him standing there, wearing nothing but his jeans and boots, a triumphant smile on his face. "Hi, Jasmine." He stepped closer to the wall and peered up at her. "The view from here is fuck-ing spectacular."

She gasped.

A crack of thunder from outside startled her and her leg trembled, her toe slipping on the ledge just as the stone she'd been clutching crumbled beneath her fingertips.

From there, everything happened in slow motion, her body barn-doored—one hand, one foot still holding on as she swung out into thin air—and then she fell.

It was only four or five feet but it seemed to go on forever.

Oomph!

Luca broke her fall, catching her shoulders so that she landed with very little impact on her feet. His look of triumph was replaced by a look of fear. "Are you okay?" He smoothed hair away from her temple. It was still tender, even after a week. "Jasmine?"

She smiled up at him. "I'm fine."

The dovecote was lit by a flash of lightning, which was quickly followed by a very close crash of thunder.

"We should—" Luca began.

Jasmine didn't wait for him to finish. She spun around, ducked out the door and sprinted toward the house.

CHAPTER THIRTEEN

WHAT WAS IT about a fleeing woman that evoked the instinct to chase? Seeing Jasmine dash across the lawn—skirt flapping, dark hair streaming out behind her—resulted in adrenaline surging through his veins followed immediately by a burst of energy. Making it almost too easy to catch up with her.

She squealed with what sounded like a mixture of fear and laughter when she glanced over her shoulder and saw how close he was. The sound only pushed him harder. He barely noticed that the skies had opened up and rain had begun—not until Jasmine slipped on the wet grass, almost losing her footing.

It was at that moment that he pounced, catching her off balance. He rolled so that when they hit the ground she landed on top of him, and before she had a chance to blink, he rolled her over beneath him, pinning her.

That didn't stop her from struggling.

Jesus Christ.

Suddenly, her body went slack.

Dammit. Had he taken this fantasy too far? "Are you okay? Did I hurt you?" he asked.

"You should let me go."

Instinctively, Luca climbed off of her and Jasmine

scrambled to her feet. Too late, he saw the gleam of mischief in her expressive eyes.

"See you, sucker!" With a squeal she took off in the other direction.

A simple lunge and he had a handful of her skirt. He yanked her into his arms, spun her around, bent down and kissed her with the ferocity that chasing her had evoked. It was while she was moaning into his mouth that he grabbed the ties from his pocket and then twisted the fabric around her wrists, tying her hands together.

"Hey, that's cheating," she complained without conviction.

"I don't recall any rules to this game other than you run and I chase."

She panted while she looked up at him, her gaze hazy with desire.

"Do you like chasing me?" she asked, glancing knowingly at the crotch of his jeans.

"Strangely…yes." Thinking the game had come to an end, Luca took Jasmine's arm and started leading her toward the villa. He glanced down. "Did you like being chased?"

"Strangely, yes." She winked, and with that, Jasmine bolted. Again.

God damn.

How had he found such a woman? Someone who matched him so well? There was nothing like it to get his blood pumping and this time when he caught her he wrapped his arms tightly around her slight body.

"Let me go." She wriggled against him, her breasts brushing against his arms, her skin hot and wet against his bare chest.

"I'm not falling for that again."

Luca held her tight with one arm while he reached around the front of her, bunching up the material of her dress in order to get underneath. He needed to touch her. He needed to know if she was as aroused by the chase as he was.

She was so turned on, her sweet pussy was weeping tears down the insides of her thighs.

Luca groaned into her hair and plunged his fingers inside of her. Jasmine keened, a primal, animal sound. Luca had heard that cry before. At least twenty times before. And he knew what it meant.

Jasmine fucking loved this as much as he did.

Luca was tempted to lay her back down on the grass and fuck her. He had a condom in his pocket and it would feel so good. For both of them. But the rain was falling in sheets and they were drenched. So, instead, Luca decided to stick to the original plan.

He pulled his hand out from between her thighs and sucked his fingers into his mouth. "You taste good, Little Red," he whispered harshly in her ear. "I can't wait to feast on you."

Her knees buckled and he caught her, throwing her up and over his shoulder.

"Let me go!" She even went so far as to pummel her small fists against his back, but the resistance was all feigned as she nuzzled her face against his bare back and licked him.

Then she bit him.

Luca held the backs of her thighs tight against his shoulder as he trudged the rest of the distance to the terrace, enjoying the feel of Jasmine's mouth on his skin. Kisses, licks and bites included. Instead of taking her to the master bedroom, where they'd spent most of their time thus far, he took her to the cellar door—that he'd made sure to leave open—and carried her down into the extensive wine cellar beneath the house. It was cool in the cellar, and Jasmine would probably feel a chill because of her wet dress.

That was fine; he'd have it off her momentarily.

The cellar was lit by every candle he'd been able to find in the house, giving it a warm and sexy glow. There was a worktable he'd set up as a tasting area and another one set against a grate on which he'd thrown a thick comforter. That was where he was going to tie her up.

But first, the dress. He fingered the zipper at her back.

"Holy shit," Jasmine whispered, gazing around at the cellar. "I like the candles. But seriously? How much wine does one person need?"

The cellar was a remnant from when his mother's family was a producer in the area. His father hadn't wanted to continue cultivating the grapes here—it wasn't champagne from the Champagne region, so what was the point?—but there were still thousands of bottles in the cellar.

Luca wasn't looking at the wine, however. He only had eyes for Jasmine. Dripping wet, hair hanging in her face, her dress now unzipped and hanging off her shoulders. She was a magnificent sight.

The only problem was, with her arms bound, he had no choice but to use a knife to slice the thick straps at her shoulders.

"Luca!" she gasped.

"Shh," he commanded. "No talking."

She blinked at him, her lips turning up in a half smile as he peeled the wet material from her body.

"Unless you want me to gag you for real."

She gnawed on her lip and shook her head.

"I am going to blindfold you. And you don't get a choice about that." Luca removed the other strip of cloth—shockingly still dry—from his pocket and placed it over Jasmine's eyes, securing it behind her head.

She made soft little sounds at the back of her throat, and Luca took an extra blanket left folded by the table and rubbed her damp skin. Taking a step back, Luca took a moment to gaze at her—her faced turned blindly toward him, her hands tied together in front of her, reaching for him.

Trusting him.

Un-fucking-believable.

Warmth infused him as he carefully untied the rope from the bindings around her wrists, picked her up— blanket and all—and laid her down on the comforter. He secured her wrists to the grate by her head. The table wasn't long enough for her entire body, ending at her knees so they bent over the edge. It was perfect for what he had in mind.

"Spread your legs," he commanded.

She shook her head.

Damn. That wasn't what he expected. He'd thought she was finished with the facade. Apparently not. But maybe this was better.

"Spread your legs, now."

A soft mewling sound slipped past her lips, but she acquiesced. Luca's dick throbbed with fierce need and he pulled out another couple of ties, eased her thighs even wider—to the accompaniment of gasps of pleasure—and tied each ankle loosely to a leg of the table.

The sight of her tied like that was almost more than he could handle.

"You shouldn't have run. You shouldn't have fought me," he said, his voice coarse.

She wet her lips before continuing to breathe through her mouth.

"You leave me no choice…" He went to the table where he'd set up four bottles of wine ranging from crisp white to thick dessert. "Now I'm going to have to punish you."

The sound of her sucking in a breath echoed against the stone walls.

"Would you like to know how I'm going to punish you?" He poured a glass from the first bottle and moved right up beside her.

Her head bobbed in a circular movement, a mixture of yes and no.

He leaned down, very close to her, and dipped his finger into the glass of wine before running it along her lips. Whispering in her ear, he said, "First I'm going to taste you." He licked the sheen of wine off her lips. "Then I'll drink from you." He poured a tiny bit of wine between her parted lips and before she could swallow, he fixed his mouth to hers and drank the wine from her mouth. "Suck you." He poured a little pool in the hollow at the base of her neck and bent to suck. Wine and flesh. So fucking delicious.

"And finally?" Luca caressed her cheek, drew his fingers down her throat, between her breasts, past her belly until his hand cupped the top of her mound. "I'm going to eat you."

* * *

It was like Luca had attached electrodes to all her best bits—her nipples, her clit, her mouth, her ass—and sent thousands of volts of electricity through her, because her entire body went rigid with the shock of desire.

Never had she imagined she could feel this way. Not even close.

He dribbled wine—a delicious white—into her mouth, down her chin and throat and across her breasts.

"I'm starting with a chenin blanc. This is a new wine I purchased in town. Fresh." He licked her neck and whispered, "Fruity." He circled her breasts. "Exquisite."

It was all made so much better by the fact she was blindfolded. *And* tied down. All she could do was lie there and feel. The pressure of his tongue, the warmth of his mouth, the abrasion from his teeth. The suction.

God.

She heard the *glug-glug* of more wine being poured—was it from a new bottle?—and then Luca moved up by her head. "Do you have any idea how hard you made me when I was chasing you?"

She shook her head.

He untied the cloth from the grate, directed her still-bound hands close to him and then placed them against his crotch. Oh! He was monstrous. Luca ground her hands against him before finally, with a groan, drawing them away. That was when he dipped her fingers into cool liquid and stuck them in his mouth. His tongue ran between her digits, lapping at her before sucking.

Hard.

His mouth was so warm and soft inside. She wanted

more but instead he stopped. She made a sound of protest but he once again tied her hands to the grate above her head, anyway.

"I think I need to torture you a little more," he whispered before dripping wine down her inner arm, catching the trail with his mouth. He poured some onto her breasts and sucked it off the sides, the place between... then right off the tips of her tight nipples.

She moaned in ecstasy when he chewed gently on those tips, like they'd been marinated.

"Do you have any idea how much I want you right now?"

"Luca," she moaned.

He pressed a finger to her mouth. "Shh. This is a sauvignon blanc from this cellar. It's fifteen years old, which some think is too old, but I think is perfect. Do you want a taste?"

She nodded, and he carefully spilled some wine into her mouth. It could have been vinegar and it still would have tasted amazing. But it wasn't vinegar. It was the most heavenly wine she'd ever tasted.

Luca moved away again and Jasmine strained to hear what he was doing. Ahh, pouring more wine. How many bottles? She couldn't remember. She'd been too taken by the fantasy of being lugged—kicking and screaming—down into a cellar by her shirtless savage.

The mere thought of the short-lived chase sent a fresh wave of blood to her clit, resulting in a heady throbbing sensation that made her writhe.

"This is one of the estate's finest. A pinot noir. There used to be many pinot grapes in the region. Now they are rare." He poured this wine on her stomach, and

Jasmine could feel it pooling in the indent of her navel and spill over her sides. "Just like you." He sipped from her skin.

He was getting so close to where she wanted him that, even with her limbs secured, Jasmine lifted her hips, forcing her midsection toward him.

"Ah...my little captive..."

Right. She was supposed to be fighting him. Well, it was her fucking fantasy. She could do whatever the hell she wanted, and right now she wanted to encourage him to suck the throbbing place between her legs that was in desperate need of release.

He slid damp fingers over her mound to the swollen flesh at the top. He pinched and she cried out. "Is this what you want Jasmine?"

She squirmed, feeling completely exposed with her legs pulled apart.

"You want me to touch you here? Pour wine over you? Suck it off you?"

She whispered, "Yes. Oh, God, yes."

But did Luca grant her wish? Maybe he wasn't a genie, after all. He poured wine on her thighs, on her belly, her knees and lapped it all up, but he avoided the place she wanted him most.

"Please, Luca," she moaned.

"Please what?"

"Please touch me."

"Like this?" He flicked his finger briefly across her clit and she moaned in frustration.

"Harder."

"Like this?" He pressed down with his thumb, moving her clit around in firm circles.

"More. Please." She was panting now. Panting because it felt so good, panting because she knew it would soon feel even better and panting because she couldn't see and had no idea what he was going to do next.

Starting at the top of her mound, something thick and cool trickled down over her clit, between her folds, and Jasmine even felt slick coolness entering her.

"This is my dessert wine. The grapes were picked by hand. It is made only for the family." He licked the spot just above her clit. "Very rare." Now he sucked her clit into his mouth. "And it's never tasted better."

With strong hands on her thighs, Luca finally bent his head to her—oh, she wished she could see. He started off gently, just making passes with his tongue. But that didn't last long. Thank God. His fingers dug into her flesh as his mouth consumed her. Licking, sucking, penetrating...

Jasmine raised her head from the bedding as if to watch. She couldn't see but her imagination filled in the blanks. Luca's thick, dark hair, bobbing between her thighs. The veins on his hands popping with the strain of holding her. A different angle now, as he moved to flick her clit with his tongue, raising his gaze to catch hers, a wicked smile in his eyes as he tortured her with his mouth.

Oh!

His mouth became brutal. Licking and biting, nipping at her folds and holding them between his teeth as he slipped a finger inside of her. Jasmine felt an orgasm building along her buttocks and spine; it was a deep one, but for some reason, she wanted to stave it off. This was all too good. It couldn't end yet.

"Come for me Jasmine. I need you to come." Luca

growled as he plunged more than one finger inside of her.

"No," she moaned, rolling her head from side to side. "Not yet."

"Yes." He slammed his fingers inside, wriggling them back and forth against her walls. "Right now."

Despite Jasmine's efforts to keep her orgasm at bay, her body had other ideas. Contractions starting from the backs of her knees joined forces with the mounting pressure at the base of her spine, tightening her abdomen and her ass, and pulling on her innards as if to bring everything inside her body together, only to blow them apart again.

But they didn't blow...not yet.

She cried out with the massive orgasm that was lurking so close to the surface. "Luca!" She screamed his name over and over again.

He grunted and stopped what he was doing.

No!

But then the ties on her legs were loosened and she could move, not that she wanted to. Then her hands were released from the grate and he tore off the other ties that had bound her hands together.

The blindfold remained.

He pulled her off the table onto her feet, turned her around and pushed down on her back, bending her over. "I need to be inside of you," he grunted.

And then he was. So fucking deep.

That's all it took for her to shatter.

Jasmine could barely support herself as her body disintegrated with pleasure while Luca drove into her from behind, again and again, harder and harder, deeper and deeper. And just when she thought she was coming down from her orgasmic rapture, Luca cried out, held her hips flush against his and erupted inside of her.

Jasmine came all over again.

CHAPTER FOURTEEN

LUCA COULDN'T REMEMBER enjoying a day so much. After the cellar, they took the opened wine bottles to the kitchen and cooked a meal together while finishing off a couple of the vintages. During dinner, he'd inquired about any other fantasies she might have hidden deep inside of that deceivingly innocent exterior.

"Well, there is this one where we're in a public place…a museum or something."

"Really?" He leaned close to kiss her neck. "You never cease to surprise."

Now they sat in the living room, a fire crackling in the fireplace to foil the dampness of the evening. There was no television, at least not a working one, and they cuddled on the couch while Luca read out loud from a book of short stories. The one he'd chosen was called, *La Vénus d'Ille*. He would read a passage in French— Jasmine had insisted, said his reading in French was turning her on—and then would translate it for her.

It was an old story about a bronze statue of Venus that was cursed, came to life and eventually killed a young man who was about to be wed by taking his wife's place in the marital bed. It ended with the statue being melted down into a bell, which then cursed the village with poor crops.

Jasmine sat up at the end of the story, a frown marring her features. "What kind of story is that?"

"A classic French tale."

"But it's so tragic."

"Not all stories have happy endings." Luca closed the book and put it down on the table.

Jasmine took his hand and threaded her fingers though his. "They should." She turned her head to him.

"Don't tell me you believe in happy endings."

"Of course I do."

He was about to say something about the fact that her engagement had not had a happy ending, but decided not to. Instead, he cupped her chin and kissed her. There was something so endearing about her optimism. Even if it was misguided.

"Luca," she said, after they broke apart. Her eyes were large and full of something that wasn't lust. For once. What was it? Curiosity? Concern?

Shit.

"I've told you all about me. I've even told you some of my darkest fantasies..." She rubbed his fingers. "But I still don't know anything about you."

She was right. He'd barely told her anything. Not about who he really was, not about why he was hiding out. He hadn't even come clean about how he'd met her. Why? Because he was still afraid she would expose him?

He wasn't afraid anymore.

"What do you want to know?"

Jasmine chewed on her bottom lip. "How about we start with this place. Who's is it, really?"

"What do you mean?"

"You know where everything is. You know all about the wine stored in the cellar. You know about the boats and the old cars in the garage and—"

"You're right," he interrupted. "This house belonged to my mother. When she and my father married, she kept this as our summer house. Every summer, I came here with her while my father worked."

"Where are your parents now?"

"Dead."

"Oh. I'm sorry." She squeezed his hand. "When did they die?"

"My father died about a year ago." He glanced around at the walls of his mother's house as if they were listening, too. "My mother died when I was sixteen. It was a car accident." He turned his gaze back to Jasmine. "I was driving."

He'd never told anyone before. It was strange how easily it came out.

"Oh, Luca. I'm so sorry."

He caught the hand that was about to stroke his cheek and held it aloft. "My father never forgave me. At least, I don't think he did. I never had the chance to ask."

"Luca…"

From somewhere down the hall, a telephone rang. It was such an out-of-place sound, both he and Jasmine jumped, as if it wasn't an everyday noise but a message from ghosts of his past.

Luca pushed off the couch and strode down the hall to where he'd left his phone in the bedroom. The call went to voice mail but he recognized the number. François.

Luca immediately called him back and heard the relief in François's voice.

"Good news," François said. "You can come out of hiding."

"What's going on?"

"Prices are up and we've pushed the date of the sale of the Legrand Goût des Rubis to tomorrow. I need you in Paris for the press conference. Show the board you can handle it and I think we can sway favor your way."

"Press conference? Wait, how do you know I'm not in Paris?"

"Luca, I've known you all my life. There's only one place you'd go after the paparazzi fiasco last week."

Of course François would know where he was. He'd worked for the family for decades.

"So," François hedged. "What did you do about the woman?"

Luca glanced toward the door. "She's still here, with me."

He could hear the disapproval dripping through the silence on the line. Finally, François said, "Press conference is at eleven tomorrow morning. You need to get rid of her by then."

"Get rid of her? What do you mean?"

"Take her to the police station. There's one a few blocks from the hotel where we're holding the conference. Let her figure it out from there. She is not your responsibility, Luca. You can't risk another scandal, not tomorrow of all days. Do you understand?"

"Of course," Luca said, though he wasn't exactly sure how Jasmine was a scandal.

He hung up the phone and stood in the dim silence of the room for a moment. This was good news. He should feel elated. He could return to his normal life, a week earlier than expected, no less. Yet it all came with a strange heaviness.

This week had been…un-fucking-believable. Jasmine was un-fucking-believable. But it wasn't real. It was just like he'd tried to explain to her not twenty minutes ago. Real life had no happily-ever-afters. Life was nothing more than a combination of events: some happy, some sad, most in-between. And then?

It all ended.

While this last week had been one of the happiest he'd ever experienced, like everything in life, it had to end.

He was taking her back to Paris. Just like that. After the most monumental day of her life…it was all coming to an end.

After the phone call, Luca had returned and proceeded to explain that he needed to return to Paris and that it was time she return to her life, too. Their "fairy tale" existence—if sex several times a day was a fairy tale—had come to an end. Then he'd taken her hand, led her to the bedroom and made love to her.

One last time.

Sometime in the night he'd gotten up and slept in the other bedroom, leaving her alone.

"What did you expect, Jazz?" she whispered to herself as she reached across the empty side of the bed. "Did you really think he'd invite you to stay? Did you think this was anything more than a holiday tryst?"

Yes.

It was true. Last night, before the phone call, Luca had finally opened up to her. For a brief moment, she'd entertained ideas about sharing a life with him. God, she was such a hopeless romantic. She'd been living in a fantasy world, and even if this fantasy world was *so* much better than any she'd been able to construct in her imagination, it didn't change the fact that it wasn't real and never had been.

After barely sleeping, Jasmine decided to get up once the sun peeked through the drapes. Time to face the day she'd secretly hoped would never come. She showered and made her way to the kitchen to start the coffee. There was an old stovetop espresso maker—a moka pot?—that made the best coffee.

She gazed around at the kitchen. Old cabinetry, an old gas stove that was finicky, a refrigerator that was barely larger than a bar-sized one she had at home.

Home?

Where the hell was her home?

She had none.

She'd lived with Parker for two years of their three-year relationship, and while his penthouse apartment was ultramodern, with all the conveniences she could ask for, she felt more at home here in this outdated kitchen than she ever had in Chicago.

"That must be the sex talking," she muttered as she turned on another burner to fry up some eggs. Luca was right. It was time she stopped avoiding her life and face what had happened back in Chicago. It was time she found herself.

The hard part was, she'd never felt more like herself than she did right here.

A noise from the hall had her turning around. Luca stood in the doorway of the kitchen. At least…she thought it was Luca.

"Your beard. You shaved it."

"Yes."

But it was more than his clean-shaven face that made him appear different. His black curls had been slicked back in a way she'd never seen before. He wore clean jeans and a button-down shirt that had been pressed. There was almost nothing about this man that resembled the sexy brute who had pursued her—and captured her—yesterday.

Nothing except his eyes.

And in those startling blue eyes that she'd come to adore was a distance that told her everything she needed to know without him having to say it.

The fairy tale was over.

She turned back to the eggs, not wanting Luca to see the emotion she feared was written quite clearly across her face. While she did that, he sliced some meat and cheese, and poured orange juice, and they sat and ate in silence. It was while they were cleaning the breakfast dishes—when had they gotten into such a familiar routine?—that Luca finally spoke.

"I left the bag on your bed so you can pack your things. We'll leave in half an hour."

Not trusting her voice, Jasmine simply nodded.

The leather satchel that Luca had brought from Paris lay open on the bed. Jasmine took her pile of clothes out of the drawer and set everything beside the bag. She spread the bag open and was about to plop her clothes inside when she noticed Luca's wallet in the bottom. She glanced toward the open door and tiptoed back to pull it shut.

Was snooping wrong at this stage of the game?

Maybe.

But Jasmine didn't care. In a couple of hours, she'd never see Luca again. She opened the wallet to the slots that held all of his credit cards and ID. The picture on the driver's license was the clean-shaven version of Luca who had appeared this morning. He had credit cards. Lots of credit cards. She pulled each one out before slipping it back inside. Then she studied his driver's license picture again.

Something was off. What was it?

Luca Legrand.

Legrand? Hadn't he said his last name was Deschamps? She checked his credit cards again. They were all in Luca Legrand's name. Why the hell had he lied to her about his last name? It made no sense.

She opened the bill compartment and pulled out the wad of cash. The man was carrying thousands of euros. Why would he need to carry so much cash when he had credit cards? And...wait...what was this lump at the very bottom of his wallet?

Jasmine fished inside and came out holding a ring between her thumb and forefinger.

Her engagement ring.

Why the hell did Luca have her engagement ring?

Who the fuck was he?

Luca found Jasmine at the front door. She wore the same outfit she'd been wearing that first day, the leather bag sat at her feet and she stared at him with a strange expression on her face.

"Are you ready?" It was a stupid question. She was clearly waiting for him.

"Luca?" she said, moving toward him.

"Yes?"

"What happened on the day you found me?"

Her question took him by surprise. It'd been a while since they'd talked about that. Luca simply reiterated the story he'd told all along about how he'd found her on the street.

"Are you sure?" she asked, gazing into his eyes, as if testing him.

"Of course I'm sure. Why?"

"It's funny. I seem to remember—vaguely—trying to sell a ring of mine." She turned her head to the other side, regarding him. "And I was wondering if you had any idea what might have happened to it?"

Fuck.

He'd forgotten all about the ring. Where had he put it? In his wallet, maybe? Luca couldn't remember. He checked his watch. It was eight thirty. It would take them two hours to get to Paris, which didn't give him much time to spare before the press conference. He didn't have time for this conversation. Particularly for the lengthy explanation that the conversation would entail. Once life got back to normal, he'd track Jasmine down and send her the ring.

Anonymously.

But right now? They had to go.

"Sorry," he said as he picked up the bag and slung it over his shoulder. "I don't know anything about a ring." He waved Jasmine out the door and locked it behind them. His bike sat waiting for them and he passed her a helmet before putting his on. She slid hers on without another word, and when she climbed on the back behind him, she held onto the leather of his jacket. Not him.

Something was up. Probably the fact that things

were over and he was being distant. But what choice did he have?

The two-hour ride back to Paris was uneventful, apart from some wet roads from yesterday's storm. Yet how different it felt from the ride out of Paris little more than a week ago. It felt more like a month, a year, a lifetime ago.

At the exit to Nemours, he slowed, turned and asked Jasmine if she needed to stop for any reason, but Jasmine just shook her head so he drove straight through. She'd been quiet the entire ride, not that they could talk while riding a motorcycle, but she seemed different. Detached.

Well, so was he.

Even when he turned onto the Avenue de la Grande-Armée, which led to the famous roundabout circling the Arc de Triomphe, Jasmine remained quiet. Barely holding on to him.

It shouldn't matter to him, he was going to be saying goodbye to her in a matter of minutes.

Yet it did.

He took Avenue Kléber to Rue de Longchamp. The 16th Arrondissement Police Commissariat was only two blocks east. Luca pulled his motorcycle up to the front of the commissariat and stopped.

"What are we doing here?"

"This is a police station. I'm dropping you off."

Luca engaged the kickstand, removed his helmet and stood. Then he took the satchel off his shoulder to pull his wallet out before handing the bag to Jasmine, who'd also gotten off the bike.

She'd taken her helmet off along with the leather jacket he'd loaned her, and she hugged the bag against her chest, as if it were a shield. "So that's it?" Her lower lip quivered. "You don't have anything else to say to me?"

What the hell was he supposed to say? I care for you more than I should? I don't want to leave you but I have to if I want my life back?

This last week with you has been the best time of my life?

Luca simply shook his head. "*Non*. I have nothing to say."

Pain flashed across her face.

"Jasmine," he said sharply and grabbed her arm. She tried to tug away but he held on. "Please understand. I'm not who you think I am."

"So, who are you?"

"It doesn't matter. But you? You are…" God. What could he tell her? The truth, for once?

"Jasmine, you have this exceptional capacity for love. You need to go and find someone who deserves you."

It was the best, most honest statement Luca was capable of making. And what did he get for his effort? A slap across the face.

He stumbled in shock and then grabbed her hand again, needing to…what? Straighten things out? Explain?

What?

"Let go of me." She tugged but he wouldn't let go.

Suddenly people were running out of the police station. Police officers had guns drawn, shouting to get down. Luca pulled Jasmine into his arms, an automatic response.

"What's going on?" she shouted.

"I don't know."

More officers, maybe ten in all, surrounded him and Jasmine. All with guns drawn. All pointing at them.

What the fuck?

"Laissez-la partir!" an officer shouted. *Let her go.*

"Luca?" She searched his face, panic written all over hers.

"It's okay. It's okay," he reassured her, though there was not one part of him that believed things were okay.

"Luca Legrand, laissez-la partir, maintenant!"

"You need to go to them," he said as calmly as possible. He dropped his arms from around her and gave her a gentle push toward the nearest officer. Jasmine glanced back with a worried expression before slowly walking away. The officer jumped up, ran to cover her and then scurried her away.

What happened next happened so fast, Luca couldn't process it. The officers pounced and he was forced onto his stomach on the pavement. A knee was pressed into his back, the cold clasp of handcuffs were forced onto his wrists and an authoritative voice said, "Luca Legrand, you are under arrest for the kidnapping of Jasmine Sweet."

CHAPTER FIFTEEN

NOTHING WAS MAKING SENSE. There were too many people surrounding her, too much chaos, all of it happening in a language she didn't understand. The next thing Jasmine knew, she was being escorted inside the police station where more officials were waiting.

"What's going on?" she asked, over and over again, but no one answered her until a female dressed in uniform approached. She had sympathetic brown eyes and brown hair pulled back into a ponytail.

"Jasmine?" she said. "My name is Danielle. Please, would you come with me?" She held out her hand as if Jasmine was supposed to take it.

"Where are we going?"

"Somewhere quiet." Her thickly accented voice was calm and soothing, and Jasmine followed the woman to a room where two male officers were seated.

"Please, sit," Danielle said, indicating one of two empty chairs. "First of all, we are so happy to find you safe and sound."

Jasmine frowned. "People knew I was missing?"

"Yes. We've all been looking for you."

Oh, shit.

"Your family has been very worried."

Oh, God. Her family. She'd meant to email her parents and then had totally forgotten. Or rather, been distracted by mind-blowing sex…

With a man who had turned out to be a cold-hearted asshole.

She was such an idiot.

"Can I speak to them? I need to speak to them."

"Of course. We will let you speak to them momentarily. But first, I need you to answer some questions, okay?"

"Okay, but…" Jasmine looked from the woman to the men. "Do you know what happened to me?" Maybe finally she'd get some answers about the theft and the concussion.

The female officer glanced at the men, giving them some kind of meaningful look. What it meant, Jasmine had no idea.

"Your belongings were turned in to the police over a week ago."

"Belongings?" The woman was speaking English but she may as well have been speaking French for all the sense she was making.

"Your bag. With your passport, ID, money and hotel key."

"You found my bag?" Jasmine said, sitting up. What a relief. She wouldn't have to contact Parker for her documents, after all.

"Yes." The woman went on to explain how the police had contacted the hotel to return her belongings after they'd been picked up from the scene of a robbery, only to find out she'd never returned. They'd used the information on her passport to contact her next of kin.

When no one had heard from her, she became a missing person. "You have become an international incident."

"Are you fu—" Jasmine stopped herself. "Are you serious?"

"Yes. Now," the woman said. "Tell us about Luca Legrand."

Jasmine had figured Luca was in trouble with the law, but this seemed a hell of a lot more serious than what she'd supposed. What had he done?

Then suddenly, she remembered what she'd found in his wallet.

"Is this about the ring? Was Luca involved in the robbery?"

"The robbery?" She shook her head. "Luca Legrand is the heir to the Legrand estate, worth billions. I doubt he'd be involved in petty theft."

Jasmine stared open-mouthed.

Billions?

The woman tilted her head in that very French way and turned to the man writing notes with a raised brow. "But then, where that man is concerned, who can be sure of anything?" She spoke softly to the two male police officers, the one who was taking notes slid the paper in front of Danielle and then the men exited the room.

Once the door was shut, Danielle found an envelope from the pile of paperwork from which she withdrew a stack of photos and slid the first in front of Jasmine. "Can you identify the man in this photo, please."

"Yes," Jasmine said slowly, it was promotional picture for the Grand Prix circuit. "It's Luca. He lied about his last name, but I saw his ID. It's Luca Legrand."

The woman nodded. "And you have been with Monsieur Legrand since you went missing?"

"Yes, but..."

"And he held you captive?"

"No."

"No?" The officer spread the other photos out across the table, in order. "I need you to describe what is happening here."

Hesitantly, Jasmine slid the photos closer and looked at the first. Then the next and the next and the next until she'd seen all twelve images.

Holy fuck.

The pictures were grainy because they'd been taken during a storm—yesterday's storm—and they told a story. A sordid story.

Dear God.

Who the hell had taken these? And how did the police get them?

It was like time-lapse photography. Luca chasing her and tackling her. Pinning her. Tying her up. Jasmine trying to escape and Luca chasing her down again. There was even a picture of him manhandling her. Then there were images of him hauling her up and over his shoulder and carrying her back to the house.

"Look," Jasmine said. "This isn't what it seems."

"Mmm." The woman gathered the photos back up into a pile. "I think this is exactly what it seems." She patted Jasmine's hand. "It is very common to feel a sense of..." She paused as if searching for a word. "*Kinship* with your kidnapper."

"Luca didn't kidnap me."

"*Mademoiselle*, I know it may seem that way. Men like Monsieur Legrand can appear charming, but—"

The woman smiled with such understanding, yet she didn't understand anything.

Jasmine put her fingers to her temples and winced as she pressed on a still tender spot. "Please, I need to explain."

"Of course. I want you to tell me exactly what happened, and I want you to start from the beginning."

Luca had no idea how long he'd been in the interrogation room. The police had confiscated his watch and everything else on his person. When they'd first shown him the pictures, he'd been too shocked to answer any questions.

Who the hell had taken those pictures? How the hell had they found him? What the fuck was he going to do now?

When he'd finally found his tongue, he'd gone over his story about fifty times with the police, explaining that Jasmine was a tourist he'd come across who'd had an accident. That he'd simply helped her and everything was consensual and that this was one big fucking mistake.

Of course they didn't believe him.

When François finally appeared. He sat down across from Luca looking ten years older than the last time he'd seen him.

"We have to stop meeting like this," Luca attempted a joke.

It did not go over well.

"I don't even know what to say," François said.

"Say you'll talk to Jasmine. Say you can get the story straight and that you can get me out of here."

François's reply was a single raised brow followed

by a sad shake of his head. He slid the pictures that had been sitting in the middle of the table toward him and went through them. Slowly.

"It's not what it looks like," Luca said to fill in the terrible silence.

François raised his gaze and then removed his glasses to clean them.

Before Luca had a chance to add anything, there was a knock on the door and François got up to open it. An officer stood outside and spoke quietly to the lawyer. Luca heard Jasmine's name mentioned but that was the extent of it.

When the conversation ended and François returned to the table, Luca noticed the door had been left open.

"She's refusing to press charges," François said, as if this was a bad thing.

Luca stood. "Then it's all over."

"No. It's not." François sighed. "The photos were sent in by an anonymous tipster. There's no stopping them being leaked to the press. Criminal investigation or not, the public has already condemned you."

Fuck.

"I don't even know what to say to you anymore. It's over, Luca. You've ruined us." He got up and walked to the door, then stopped to say, "Oh, and the American woman wants to talk to you, apparently. She'll be here shortly."

Luca stood, scrubbing a hand up and down his face. How could things have gone so awry? There was only one way. He'd been set up. Again. And there was only one man who would do it.

Marcel.

Luca kicked the wall in anger just as the door opened. Jasmine stood there accompanied by a female officer.

"I'd like to speak to him alone, please," Jasmine said to the other woman.

"I don't think—"

"Please."

"Okay, but I'll be right outside if you need me." It was clear by the woman's tone that she didn't like the idea of Jasmine being in a room alone with him. Based on the fucking photos, he couldn't blame her.

"Jasmine," Luca began. "Thank you for—"

She stopped him with a fierce look before he could say another thing.

"Why did you lie?"

"About what?"

She threw her head back and laughed. There was not one whit of humor in it. "Let's see, about your name. About who you really are. About this…" she shoved her hand into her pocket and pulled out her ring.

Fuck.

"Jasmine, let me explain. Please."

"You had plenty of time to explain." She paced the room. "Days to explain." She stopped. "I asked you point-blank this morning about my ring and you lied to my face." She came to stand right in front of him. "Why?" She narrowed her gaze. "Did you rob the store and knock me out and then try to hide that fact by whisking me away?"

"No. God, no. That's not what happened."

"Then for the final time, tell me the truth about what happened. You've got two minutes or I press charges for theft." She tapped her toe, a permanent scowl on her face.

Luca began slowly, explaining how he'd stopped the robbery that day. How she'd chased him out of the store and he didn't know why. How she'd collapsed. How he'd found the ring later and had planned to return it. How he'd been lying low because of previous scandals he'd been involved in and that he was in danger of losing his family fortune. There was so much that it all became tangled together in his explanation.

And it all sounded terribly lame.

"So, your name is really Luca Legrand and you are heir to the Legrand champagne estate?"

"Yes. You've heard of me?"

She made a face. "The police were kind enough to explain a few things to me." She walked straight up to him and poked him hard in the chest. "Here's what they were unable to explain. Why you didn't trust me with the truth."

He'd never seen her angry. It was a sight to behold. "Jasmine. I couldn't tell you the truth. I had to lie."

"That's bullshit."

"You don't understand. I was afraid of—"

"Of what? Huh?" She poked him harder. "What the hell were *you* afraid of?"

"This." He waved to the room, the pictures, the police station at large. "I was afraid something like this might happen. Everything was at stake, my reputation, my inheritance. Everything. And, based on what has happened to me this year, I couldn't trust anyone. Not even you."

She shoved him. "And it made no difference to you that I told you *everything* about me? That I trusted you enough with *my* secrets. That I let you tie me up, for fuck's sake? But you couldn't even tell me your real name?"

"Jasmine…"

She took a step back and cocked her head to one side. "You know what, Luca," she said. "You're no better than Parker, using me so that you wouldn't lose your trust fund." She closed her eyes and lifted her chin. "Jesus," she muttered to the ceiling.

"I never used you."

"No?" Her laugh was an angry sound. "You're saying you *didn't* use my body for your own pleasure? You *didn't* use my company to make your exile more palatable?" She shook her head.

Luca had had enough of being misunderstood. "You're accusing *me* of using *you*?" he snarled in frustration. "What about you? *You* blackmailed me so I'd agree to take you with me to the villa. *You* showed up naked in my shower. It was *you* who asked me to do all of those things to your body." He grabbed her shoulders. "I didn't ask for any of that, Jasmine. It was all you."

Jasmine's mouth hung open in shock. She blinked. When she spoke, it was slowly and carefully. "Are you saying you were just doing me a favor? That you fucked me out of pity?"

Her lip quivered.

Luca's anger dissolved the second he saw tears welling up in her eyes. "No. That's not what I'm saying."

She backed away, holding her hands up as if he was an evil entity and she needed to ward him off. "You're an even bigger asshole than Parker." She spun around and marched to the door, banging on it with her fist to get the officer's attention.

"Jasmine, wait," he called. "I'm sorry."

She walked out the door and slammed it behind her, and that was when Luca realized something.

Something huge.

He didn't want Jasmine to think that he was the fuckup everyone else in the world thought he was. He wanted to go back to the villa, to the times when she'd gazed at him like he was the most amazing man in the world.

And most of all, Luca realized that he didn't care about losing everything. But he did care about losing Jasmine.

CHAPTER SIXTEEN

WHEN JASMINE FLEW back to America, she didn't even stop in Chicago but flew directly to Denver to be with her parents. She didn't plan on staying long, just until she could figure out the shit show that was her life. She also flew home to hide. Her sex-venture in France had become international news. Big in Europe first, because of the Legrand family fame, then across the Atlantic, when it became known an American was involved. Pictures of her being chased and carried off by Luca were all over social media, and since no one knew the full story, the public was left to interpret what was really happening in the condemning photos. Blog posts and new memes showed up daily, with sometimes corny but mostly offensive captions. If she thought her experience with Parker had been humiliating, she was sorely mistaken.

She now understood the true definition of humiliation.

Which made speaking to Parker somehow more bearable. She'd finally phoned him and asked him to ship her belongings, and she had to admit, he'd been accommodating. At least he wasn't still suggesting they work it out between them. She'd offered him his ring back. He refused to take it, at first, but she'd insisted.

Jasmine had to make it on her own. No more relying on men. Especially if they were only capable of lying to her. The truth was, she'd finished being angry with Parker a long time ago. Luca had helped with that. Had made her feel things she'd never thought possible. Now she was only upset with herself. She was the one who'd fallen twice for men who'd deceived her.

She was afraid her infamy would hurt her job prospects, but she got a job at the first hair salon she applied to. Once word got out about who she was (Luca Legrand's scandalous sex slave) she was booked solid for the next six months. So the upside of her disgrace was that her income was guaranteed and she would be able to move out of her parents' house sooner rather than later.

Her second week on the job, one of her coworkers came running back to her chair while she was cutting an elderly lady's hair.

"Jasmine! That guy who abducted you is on TV. Come see."

She'd given up setting people straight about her supposed kidnapping. No one listened because fiction was way more interesting than fact.

When Jasmine rounded the corner where the overhead television was perched, one of the girls turned up the volume just as Luca took the microphone in what appeared to be a press conference.

"God, he's hot. I wouldn't say no if he kidnapped me."

A rumble erupted in the pit of her stomach but she didn't say anything because she wanted to hear what

Luca had to say. He spoke in French and it was trans-
lated by a female. It started with something about the
sale of a rare bottle of champagne that had sold to
a collector for half a million euros. The man who'd
purchased the wine stood up and nodded as he was
presented with a bottle amid the flash of numerous
cameras.

Once the clamor died down, there was silence. Luca
paused, seeming to weigh his words. Then he spoke
some more. The translator seemed caught off guard and
spoke quickly to keep up. "The Legrand champagne
estate has been run by Legrand men for many genera-
tions, and while I am the last Legrand…" Luca glanced
at a man sitting beside him. "I will be resigning as CEO
and announcing a successor as soon as possible." There
was a flurry of flashing cameras, and the crowd grew
louder as reporters vied for further comments.

Jasmine frowned.

Luca was giving up his birthright? Why?

Then Luca raised his hand for silence and began
speaking in English.

"And now, I have a message for Jasmine Sweet."

O-oh, shit.

There were gasps from the other women in the salon
who had gathered round.

"Quiet," Jasmine said. "I can't hear."

Someone turned up the volume as Luca began to
speak. "Jasmine, there are so many things I regret. I regret that you have been the subject of this malicious international media frenzy. I regret lying to you. I regret
some of the things I said and some of the things I did."

Flashes went off in his face and he turned away
for a moment before continuing. "But there are many

things I do not regret. I will never regret the time we spent together. I certainly do not regret the things we did together. Most of all, I do not regret falling in love with you."

The salon went silent. All eyes turned to her.

The press conference was a nightmare, even worse than the last two weeks with relentless paparazzi hounding him. He couldn't believe what he'd just done. Yet Luca felt a strange lightness after announcing that he would be stepping down as head of the family business.

It wasn't planned. He was supposed to show up today and announce the new owner of the rare Legrand vintage. Then he'd been going to use the press conference to tell Jasmine he was sorry and that he loved her. He was sure she'd hear him this way. But as he'd stood onstage, thinking about that love, of all the things he wanted to give her, he knew she was his only priority now.

Even over his family legacy.

He refused to subject her to any more of Marcel's vindictive machinations and there was only one way to accomplish that.

Quit. So he did…on television, before he could change his mind. Now Marcel would have no reason to make his life, and Jasmine's by proxy, a living hell.

The thought of Marcel winning should have angered Luca, but he only felt relief.

Luca had just stepped into his office when Marcel appeared. "What the hell was that?" he asked, his voice angry and clipped.

Luca was too exhausted to fight with his half brother. "You have outplayed me at every turn. Take the position—it's yours. And if you want to contest the will? Go ahead."

"What are you talking about?"

"I know what you've been up to. Arranging the scandals, the paparazzi at the worst possible moments. Having me followed. Taking those pictures. You won, Marcel. At least be gracious in victory."

Marcel shook his head. "Luca, I don't know what you think I did, but I would never try to ruin you like that."

"Of course you would. You knew the board wanted you to lead the company and that the only way to do that was by contesting my inheritance. I'm just saving us all time and lawyers' fees."

"What are you talking about? Your father wanted *you* to run the company. It's yours, Luca. He already made generous provisions for me."

Luca stared hard at the man he'd blamed for his misfortune. What surprised him was how genuine Marcel appeared. Luca ran his fingers through his too-long hair. "But if you didn't do it, who else would—" Just then, François walked into the room with Marcel's fiancée, Lydia Fournier. Now Luca realized why he'd recognized her last name, she went by her mother's.

And her mother was François's ex-wife.

Lydia Fournier was François's estranged daughter. Though, by the looks of things, she was not so estranged now.

"It was you," Luca said, striding up to François. "You're the only one who knew where I was. Both times. All the time." He blinked, dumbfounded. "It was you all along."

There was a gasp from Lydia who released her father's arm as she eyed the two men in shock.

Luca turned and paced, his fingers threaded through his hair. "I trusted you. I confided in you. And you betrayed me."

"You're mistaken." François's voice was eerily calm. "It is you who betrayed your family name." He shrugged. "I just made sure the world saw you for who you truly are."

"Oh, my God." Luca stumbled backward as if François had pushed him. "Why would you do that?"

"Do you know what I have done for this company? The long hours. Being your father's right-hand man for thirty years. I gave up my own family for yours. My wife left me, my only daughter wouldn't talk to me for years." He adjusted his glasses. "Then you came along. Luca Legrand, the prodigal son who never gave a damn about the company. You were going to destroy everything I worked for. Everything I sacrificed." He shook his head. "I couldn't let it happen. So, I destroyed you, instead."

"Papa!" his daughter cried as she leaned against Marcel.

"I did it for you, Lydia." Finally he looked at his daughter.

She shook her head and clutched Marcel, who stared at the lawyer in disbelief.

"François," Luca said. "You're fired."

"You can't fire me. You're no longer in charge."

"François," Marcel said, stepping forward. "You're fired."

It had been three days since she'd seen Luca on TV and Jasmine couldn't stop thinking about him. He loved her? How could that be?

Did she love him?

Yes, of course you do, stupid.

"I can't believe he gave up all that money for you," her friend Ashley said via FaceTime. "It's so romantic. We're talking billions of dollars here, people."

"I doubt he gave it up for me," Jasmine said, waving off her friend's comment. "I'm sure he was forced to."

"Well, he certainly wasn't forced to profess his love for you in front of millions of viewers worldwide." Ashley wagged her brows suggestively.

Jasmine shook her finger at the camera. "Don't you have a baby to go birth?"

Ashley lowered the camera to show off her stomach. "Yep, overdue by three days." She groaned. "I'm about ready to explode." She raised the camera again. "Now, stop changing the subject. When are you heading back to France to snatch up that smoking-hot Neanderthal?" She tapped something on her phone and suddenly a meme popped up on Jasmine's messenger app. It was the picture of Luca carrying her over his shoulder, but instead of clothes they were dressed in hides like cavemen, with the caption *Why Luca Legrand's dating profile says Old-Fashioned.*

"Very funny," Jasmine said. "I don't think I want to be your friend anymore."

"You have to. You're going to be my baby's godmother. Now answer the question."

"I'm not going back to Paris. I've got a very good job here in Denver and I don't need a man to take care of me."

"Uh-huh. But he did take care of you, right? Like all of your nasty lady needs were *well* taken care of?"

"Okay, horny pregnant person, some of us have to go to work now. Bye!"

She ended the call before Ashley delved any deeper into how she really felt. Which was...confused.

During Jasmine's break she went to the deli next door to buy a sub, and when she got back, the receptionist stopped her. "Package for you, Jazz." The woman gave her a curious smile.

Jasmine took the package into the staff room and opened it while she ate her lunch. It was a rectangular wooden box about the size of a small toaster with a sliding lid. There were no markings on the box, nothing. Inside was something shiny and heavy. She pulled it out. It was a silver oil lamp, like the one she'd seen in the shop in Paris that fateful day. She dumped the box to see if there was a note. Nothing.

After finishing her sandwich, she washed up and went back to her station. A man with shoulder-length hair wearing a leather jacket sat in her chair with his back to her. She stopped in shock. She recognized that jacket.

Luca.

"What the hell are you doing here?" she asked, a mixture of relief, rage, surprise and pleasure making her voice sound weird.

He turned in the chair. She'd forgotten how startlingly blue his eyes were. Well, she hadn't forgotten, they were just so much more striking in real life than in her imagination.

"I need a haircut. Obviously."

She took a couple of steps closer and pulled her scissors out of the jar of disinfectant. "And you trust me to be near you with a sharp object?"

"I absolutely trust you," he said with a soberness that made her cheeks tingle.

"Okay. I'll cut your hair. But that's it."

"That's all I asked for."

It took her twenty minutes to do the job, and she couldn't decide if it was the longest or the shortest twenty minutes of her life. He smelled so good and he was so close, and with every snip of her scissors, memories flickered in and out of her mind's eye, making it difficult to keep her lines straight.

"There," she said as she dusted hair off his shoulders. Oh, she'd forgotten how lovely and broad his shoulders were.

The bastard.

"You look a little less like a Neanderthal now." The meme that Ashley sent her that morning flashed behind her lids and she suppressed a smile.

"Did you get my package?"

"The lamp? Yes. Are you here to grant me more wishes? Because I don't want any more."

He stood. Another thing she'd forgotten. How tall he was. He was imposing and…gorgeous.

It took her breath away.

"No. I'm not here to grant wishes. I'm here to ask *you* to grant *me* three wishes."

"Why on earth would I—"

He stopped her with a quick kiss. It was nothing compared to the searing ones he'd bestowed often during her stay at the villa, but it still resulted in her knees turning to pudding.

"All I ask is that you listen. You may decide about granting them after."

"Fine." She waved for him to proceed, hoping to hide the fact that she was finding it hard to breathe.

"First, I wish for you to return to Paris." He pulled a ticket from his pocket. "There is so much you missed, so much I want to show you. So much I think you would love."

She took the proffered ticket with exaggerated reluctance and placed it on the counter of her workstation.

"Second, I wish for forgiveness. I said and did many things I regret. I would like a chance to make it up to you."

She opened her mouth but he held up his hand before she could speak. "Let me finish." His chest rose and fell as he took a deep breath and released it. "I wish for you to tell me if my love for you is reciprocated or not."

He pressed a finger to her lips. "Don't answer now. Take your time." He handed her a small envelope. "Here are instructions if you should choose to use the ticket. The flight leaves in four days."

Luca leaned forward and kissed her softly once more, whispering in her ear. "Oh, and you may want to destroy those instructions after reading. They are for your eyes only."

When he walked out the door, every pair of eyes in the salon watched him go.

Jasmine's hand shook as she opened the envelope. She skimmed over the message once and then read it again, slowly. As she reread it for the third time, her heart fluttered in her throat when she reached the last line.

Panties optional.

CHAPTER SEVENTEEN

WOULD SHE SHOW? Luca's doubts far outweighed his confidence. He was also taking a big risk—no, a huge risk—by suggesting this rendezvous. But if there was one thing he'd learned, Jasmine was worth the risk.

Thankfully, the paparazzi weren't quite as fierce as they had been a few weeks ago. There was always a new scandal somewhere for them to prey upon. Besides, his televised declaration of love seemed to have swayed public opinion, especially when it'd been followed up with an announcement that he'd be running the estate, after all…with his *brother*. Now the world knew there were *two* Legrand heirs.

He waited in the shadows of salon five in the Musée d'Orsay, the old train station in Paris that had been converted into a museum. It was not nearly as large as the Louvre, and it was much quieter. A necessity for what he had in mind.

He checked his watch. It was five minutes past the appointed afternoon time. And then it was ten.

Fifteen.

She wasn't coming.

Suddenly a woman appeared in the entrance of the salon. She wore a red dress—bless her heart—a black bag over her shoulder and black heels that did amazing things to her already shapely legs. Her dark hair fell in stylish waves past her shoulders. She stopped inside the salon, glanced around, referred to a pamphlet in her hand and moved inside.

She stood in front of *L'âge d'or: La nuit* by Léon Frédéric, just as Luca had instructed. He'd chosen this salon for its remoteness in the museum.

He walked up behind her quietly, hoping she wouldn't hear him.

However, perhaps she felt his presence, as he did hers, because as soon as he was within earshot, she spoke. "Americans should adopt the European attitude toward the naked body." Her voice was low and husky.

"Do you think so?"

"Oh, yes. We're much too uptight." She tilted her head to take a better look at the rendition of a group of people, mostly naked, sleeping together in a field. "The human body is very beautiful."

He brushed hair from her shoulder. "*You* are very beautiful," he said softly against her skin. Then he raised her chin and turned her toward him.

Her eyes were large and liquid as she gazed up at him.

"I'm so glad you're here."

She blinked and he felt her soft breath on his cheek. "You're a hard man to say no to, Luca Legrand."

Relief filled him. "I hope that's a good thing."

"Sometimes." She smiled up at him.

He recognized that smile. A lethal mixture of sensuousness and innocence.

His relief grew. "I would like to thank you for making the trip."

She bit down on her lower lip. "How would you go about doing that? Thanking me?"

"There are so many ways, Jasmine." It was true. He wanted to be so many things to this woman. Her lover, yes, but more, too. He wanted to be the man she woke up to, the man she shared her fears and hopes and dreams with. He wanted to laugh with her, cook with her, read books together on a cozy couch. He wanted to share his life with her.

While her presence suggested much, he needed desperately to know that she believed in him and there was only one way to find out.

"Do you trust me?"

She crossed her arms over her chest. "I don't know, you've given me very little reason to trust you." She shifted from one foot to the other. "Why?"

While she was playing it cool, Luca could feel the warmth emanating from her skin, telling him that she already knew where this was going. He had been explicit in his letter…

He leaned close and whispered in her ear. "There is a fantasy of yours I would very much like to fulfill."

Breath stuttered inside her throat. "Oh?" She was trying to sound coy. It was so fucking sweet.

"But it requires trust." He paused. "Can you forgive me enough to place your trust in me?"

She blinked up at him, carefully considering his question. Good, because it was critical to him that she knew what she wanted. What he wanted.

"Please?"

"O-kay…"

Relief washed over him and Luca curbed the urge to shout with joy. Instead, he took her hand and led her into an even smaller and quieter gallery adjacent to the one they'd just been in. Luca directed her to the corner, so she was standing behind a display of a statue and he stood close behind her, their backs to the wall. "Look at the sculpture. Read the inscription."

"But I can't read French…"

His hand slid beneath the hem of her skirt, moving upward. "Try. Say it out loud."

"Um… Jean Hugues…" Her breath caught as his fingers explored higher: her thighs, her bare ass—Jesus!—the front of her.

"Luca?" She glanced over her shoulder. "Are you sure?"

"Shh," he whispered. "Spread your legs, lean forward and keep reading."

Instead of words, a soft gasp slipped out of her mouth.

The result was a fierce tightening in his groin. "There is no one else in this room. The light is dim. No one can see." He was barely touching her, yet he could feel heat on the inside of her thighs and her skin was lightly damp. "Read."

"Torse de jeune-…" She grunted when he delicately parted her soft lips.

"Go on," he murmured, pressing his fingertips into her warm core.

"Fille." She angled her head. "I'm not saying that right, am I?"

"You're doing fine." His other hand slid beneath her hair and around her neck as two fingers slid deeper inside of her.

"What…what does that mean?" She panted.

"Torse de jeune-fille means torso of a young girl."

Curving his fingers, he pressed against the satiny walls of her channel.

"Ahhh…" Her back arched as she raised her ass into his hand.

"Tell me, do you like being fingered in public?"

"Yes." She rocked back into him.

"Are you worried someone will see?" He withdrew his fingers from her heat and rubbed the moisture across her pussy and clit before playing around the tight little opening of her ass.

"Maybe…but…no. Not really," she said, followed by a soft whine.

Christ. So many things he still wanted to do with this woman. She was so willing and passionate and ravenous in her sexual appetite.

And she was here. She'd come. That had to mean something. She wouldn't have come all this way just for sex. It had to mean more.

It did for him.

A man walked into the room, glanced in their direction and then moved to study the Renoir near the entrance. Jasmine squeaked softly against his palm.

"Shh," he murmured in her ear. His hand drifted from her mouth to her jaw and down to her shoulder where he brushed hair away to place a soft kiss on her bare skin.

"Luca." His name was a soft moan.

"I'm not going to stop until you come." He nibbled her ear. "I want your come in the palm of my hand."

His comment resulted in her grinding into his hand.

"This sculptor? Jean Hugues? How do you think he knows a woman's torso so well?" He paused, even though he didn't expect an answer. "By touching her."

He rubbed her fat little clit with his thumb while he vibrated his fingers inside of her. "Caressing her." While his hand on her shoulder and throat was gentle, the one beneath her skirt was not. "He probably fucked her in every way possible," he whispered softly in her ear.

The low whine, which Luca had come to learn meant she was close, started deep in her chest.

"Shh, *ma colombe.*" He rubbed his jaw against her hair while he placed his palm flat between her legs, cupping her. "You need to keep quiet when you come."

Her whole body flinched within the circle of his arms and a surge of moisture filled his hand.

"Yes, just like that." He buried his face in her hair. "Luca." She clung to him and he loved it. God he loved it.

In fact, he loved it so much—loved her so much— he swept the hair away from her ear and told her how he felt.

Oh. My. God. She'd had an orgasm in a museum. With other people in the room. It was…unbelievable! But even better—like a billion times better—was the fact that Luca had told her that he loved her.

And this time she believed him.

After the museum, Luca took her to the Eiffel Tower and they went up to the top where a wind gust threatened to expose her, literally, to the world. As if she hadn't been exposed enough in the last month. But none of that mattered anymore because she was here, at the Eiffel Tower, not gazing at it from a balcony alone but sharing it with the man she loved.

It made all the difference.

Once they were back down on the ground, Luca

unpacked a picnic lunch and spread everything on a blanket on the grass. Before he let her sit, however, he wrapped his arms around her, held her close and whispered wonderful things in her ear.

Not naughty things—well, there may have been a couple of naughty suggestions—but mostly it was about how he felt about her. How scared he'd been that she wouldn't show today. How he wanted to make her dreams come true, and her fantasies—like they'd just done. But mostly he wanted to prove to her that this was about more than sex.

It was about connection and understanding and about two people who trusted one another.

She turned in his arms and linked her hands around his neck. "Luca?"

"Yes?"

"I forgive you."

"Really?"

"Yes."

"That simple?"

"Um…you call confessing your love on international TV, giving up your inheritance, flying across the country to give me a lamp and then flying me here, simple?"

He laughed. "Well, when you put it that way…"

She went up on tiptoes and kissed him soundly on the mouth. Then she tilted her chin up and said, "By the way, I love you, too."

He whooped at the sky, then picked her up and spun her around.

"Careful," she squealed so he'd set her down. She patted her skirt into place. "I'm not wearing anything under this, remember?" She laughed, wondering at how life could change. Luca brought out extremes of emotions, from the most pleasure she'd ever experienced to the greatest anger. In between those extremes, her heart had ached for him. All of it, all of the emotions— even the extremes—made her feel more alive than she'd ever felt.

They sat down and shared a lunch of bread, cheese, wine and pastries gathered from local shops. They were *not* the only picnickers in the park and Luca borrowed a corkscrew from a neighboring group.

God, she loved Paris. The people were so uninhibited.

Here she was drinking wine in a public place after being fingered in a public place, hanging out with a rich and famous man in a public place.

This was living.

"You're smiling."

"I'm happy." She gazed at him. "Thank you for inviting me here." She covered his hand. "And thank you for…" She bit her lip. "Saying what you said in the press conference. I hope you didn't really give everything up for me."

"Of course I did." He grinned and there was a flash of mischief in his eyes. "But, as it turns out, my brother is a better man than I am. I'd intended to make him CEO, but we have decided to run the company together." He took a drink of wine and a far-off look came into his eyes. "It's what my father would've wanted."

"Oh, Luca." She leaned over and kissed him.

He kissed her back with the freedom and joy of a Parisien in love.

"However, I have a new venture I am thinking about." He stroked her cheek. "Though I need a partner."

"Oh?"

"Yes. I want to market my mother's wines again. It's the area I love. The wines I love. It is a shame to let those vines go to waste."

"That sounds like an amazing idea."

"Yes. I think so." He took her free hand. "And I'm wondering if you would consider being my partner in that venture?"

She sat up, stunned. "You want me to come back to the villa?"

"Yes. It will be hard work and it may not be your passion, becoming a vintner. So, give yourself some time—"

"Yes!" Jasmine threw her arms around him before he could finish. "Yes, of course, yes." She smiled up at him. What he was asking her was so different from a man telling her he wanted to take care of her.

Being partners? That sounded like a dream come true. "From the very first, that place seemed more like home to me than anywhere else I've ever lived."

"It's not too...provincial?"

"No. I love it there."

"Bien." He handed her wine back to her and they clinked glasses. "You may have to learn French."

"J'ai déjà commencé." I've already started.

Jasmine smiled broadly at Luca's look of surprised approval. Then she squirmed when he whispered something about looking forward to teaching her more intimate French things while he inched his hand up beneath her skirt.

She playfully slapped his hand away and rearranged her skirt, grinning. Then Jasmine reclined so that she could put her head in Luca's lap.

"I told you," she said softly, eyes closed.

"Told me what?"

"That happy endings make the best stories."

She opened her eyes to find Luca gazing down at her with adoration in his eyes. *"Touché,"* he whispered.

* * * * *

LET'S TALK
Romance

For exclusive extracts, competitions
and special offers, find us online:

- facebook.com/millsandboon
- @millsandboonuk
- @millsandboon

Or get in touch on 0844 844 1351*

For all the latest titles coming soon, visit
millsandboon.co.uk/nextmonth